ff

EMMA TENNANT

Queen of Stones
and
Alice Fell

faber and faber
LONDON · BOSTON

Queen of Stones was first published in 1982
by Jonathan Cape Ltd, London
and later in a paperback edition
by Pan Books Ltd, London
Alice Fell was first published in 1980
by Jonathan Cape Ltd, London
and later in a paperback edition by
Pan Books Ltd, London

This paperback edition first published in 1987
by Faber and Faber Ltd
3 Queen Square London WC1N 3AU

Printed and bound in Great Britain by
Cox & Wyman Ltd, Reading
All rights reserved

British Library Cataloguing in Publication Data

Tennant, Emma
Queen of stones; and Alice fell.
I. Title   II. Tennant, Emma.
823'.914[F]   PR6070.E52
ISBN 0–571–14814–X

QUEEN OF STONES

For Laura Mulvey
with love

Missing Girls – Fears Grow

Fears grow for the safety of a group of young girls who set out on Friday on a sponsored walk from Beaminster to Melplash (on footpaths via Mapperton) and who have since mysteriously disappeared, after being spotted by a helicopter pilot on Friday afternoon.

They were going downhill towards the coast at Abbotsbury, reported pilot Jimmy Carr, and he had thought they were local girls on the way home from school, although they were in fact miles off course. 'There was a bunch of them walking quite fast so they seemed to know where they were going,' said Carr, who was at the time on the way back from a cliff rescue call in the area. 'I had no idea they were lost or I'd have come down.'

Asked by police if he could identify any of the girls from photos, Carr said he could be definite about only one, tall red-haired Bess Plantain, daughter of Mr Plantain of Forton Court. He was equally sure, however, that she wasn't wearing the clothes she was said to have set out in. 'I don't know about a skirt or jeans or whatever, but she wasn't in a Shetland knit,' Carr said firmly. He went on to describe a white ruffled blouse, see-through and with high flounces at the neck. 'You couldn't miss it,' said Carr before going on to reveal another surprise to reporters. 'A dark girl brought up the rear, I can swear to that,' insisted the pilot after looking through all the photographs and identification provided. 'And she wasn't one of these.'

Parents are meeting this evening to discuss future steps in the investigation and to question Mr Carr further on the apparent direction of the girls at the time of the sighting.

I

The girls have by now spent two nights (presumably) in the open, while search parties, held back by the worst fog on the West Dorset coast since the first weather recordings, have failed to come up with any clues.

The walk, organised by the Women's Legion Committee, was under the leadership of Jane Stretherick, 52. 'Everyone was waiting in the village hall at Melplash,' said a weary and emotional Miss Stretherick at the bungalow home she shares with her parents at West Bay earlier today. 'It was going to be tea and dancing after the walk. Then, the fog came down – we all got separated. I found myself alone, climbing up through the gardens of Parnham House before I could get on the road to Beaminster. Somehow I groped my way to the main square and banged on the door of the Red Lion to let me in.'

While Jane Stretherick rested in the comfort of the thirteenth-century Red Lion, her group wandered further afield. There are now fears that, in the dense fog, they may have fallen from the cliffs (if they ever reached the coast road). The Women's Legion Central Committee has sent messages of concern to the parents of the children, and an extra assignment of police is expected to arrive from Dorchester later today, to widen the search for the girls.

Missing are: Bess Plantain (13) and her sister Jane (11) of Forton Court, Melplash. Bess attends Ferndale School for Girls, where Jane is due to join her next term on leaving the local primary, St Jude; Mary and Mathilda Barton (also 11), twin daughters of J. H. Barton, teacher at Melplash Comprehensive; Melanie Ayres (9) of Whitehays Estate (St Jude); Nat Minges (8) of Bay Cottage near Waytown, daughter of the late Bob Minges, one of the lifeboatmen drowned in the Poole Harbour disaster in 1979.

The whole of Class Four from Melplash Primary were also on the walk. The average age is six years, two months. 'I feel most concerned,' Mr Ralph Plantain of Forton Court (whose two girls are amongst the missing) told us today in the book-lined study of gracious Forton Court, home of the Plantain family for over a hundred years. 'I feel my own girls can look after themselves. Bess is a sensible thirteen-year-old and Jane has been a terrifically active personality since she was small. But the young members of Class Four – I would like to express my deepest sympathy with their parents – and indeed the parents of all the missing girls – and ask them to join us in a fervent prayer for their safe return.'

As darkness comes down once more, anxieties are likely to treble if the girls are not found safe and sound. Mr J. H. Barton, father of missing twins Mary and Mathilda, suggests going along the fog-bound coast in a boat and, with the aid of powerful lights, picking out the girls if they should have come to harm on the beach or at the foot of the cliffs. Mrs Minges, mother of eight-year-old Nat, is adamant, however, that her daughter would take fright if this form of rescue were attempted, and might infect the others with her panic. And memories of the lifeboat disaster are too strong in local memory to encourage such a venture.

Author's Note

At the time of the 'Isle of Portland tragedy', I was staying with friends near by; I was recovering from an illness and had time on my hands: hence the decision to make an attempt to reconstruct the strange happenings of the week-end of October 17, 1981. These happenings, which were that a violent death had taken place amongst a group of girls in West Dorset that week-end and that none of the participants (or spectactors – it was impossible to tell which was which) would give any coherent account of the subject, prompted me to try to obtain all relevant information on the group of girls, and to write an 'imaginative reconstruction' of events. The result is presented, very tentatively, in this book. Tentative it must remain: even if I have succeeded in compiling a rough sort of dossier on the girls and their actions (from a psychiatrist, a social worker, the girls' own fragments of speech, notes and journals), it's possible to say one can learn just as much from the family snaps, blurred and casual, handed in by distraught parents to the press. A part of the truth is here, I hope; and just as a photograph may remind one person of the subject and another person not at all, it must also be understood that a 'real' sequence of happenings, quite different from my reconstruction maybe, will possibly one day come to light.

Before beginning on the afternoon of the walk organised by Miss Stretherick on behalf of the Women's Legion, we might do well to take a look at these photographs. Perhaps we can decipher from the faces of the girls what more sophisticated techniques cannot tell us. We have noted, too, the casual (yet frequently valuable) observations made about the girls by those who hardly knew them.

Bess Plantain is shown in a colour Polaroid snap taken the summer before these disastrous events. She is tall for her age – then twelve – and exceptionally good-looking, with long reddish-gold hair and a face (turned half to camera, as it is) that seems an intriguing mixture of arrogance and childish insecurity. Her eyes are bluish-green, and she has the beginnings of a woman's figure, which is well accentuated by a white blouse, almost diaphanous and with a high ruffle of lace at the neck. According to one or two village dwellers, she 'thinks too much of herself'; according to others, she is 'practical and always willing to help out'.

Bess's younger sister Jane could be said to be her exact opposite. She is leggy and thin: we see her holding the reins of a pony; she stares impatiently at the camera as if she has little time for this kind of thing. Hair, bright, dark brown and slightly curly; face, sharp and angular, more developed than the face of her elder sister, and with a small, upward-tilting nose. Comments: 'Jane's a regular tomboy.' 'Never seen her in a skirt or dress.' Jane also stutters – and quite badly. Comments on this showed embarrassment, and no observer could remember if the stutter had been there since infancy or if it had been recently acquired.

Mary and Mathilda Barton, eleven-year-old twin daughters of the maths and history master at Melplash Comprehensive, present an almost eerie picture, in the battered black and white snap dug out with difficulty by their father (the mother abandoned the family when they were under five years old, and it was evident that Mr Barton had been too busy in the intervening years to record the progress of his children). It is as if the shutter of the camera, when pressed, had somehow slipped, to produce the same image twice over, so identical are the twins in expression and stance. They are small, and would appear much less than eleven years of age if it were not for the slightly malevolent look imprinted on their faces. General colouring – hard to tell, but they seem mousy, as if hair, skin and eyes are all of one, rather worn pigment. Comments: 'They keep themselves to themselves,' 'clever, but that's the father in them,' 'keen to get on and show they can do better.'

Nat Minges, aged eight, is shown to us in the most perplexing picture of the group. A water-colour, not a photograph (her mother explained that she detests photography), gives a dreamy-looking child, extremely idealised – it is the work of the mother, and Nat is painted as a fairy, complete with gauzy wings and a cap of petals – in a woodland glade, with various symbols of her interests at her feet; ammonites, wild flowers, etc. She appears stranger in appearance in this picture than she is in fact, being a straightforward, pleasant-faced little girl with, it is true, a faraway look in her eyes. Comments: 'Nat hasn't been herself since she lost her father at sea.' 'That girl's mother ought to have more sense than to fill her little head with all that fairy stuff.' 'If you meet Nat she'll look straight through you, as if she's looking at someone else.'

Melanie Ayres is available to us only in a group photograph, taken in July on the last day of term at St Jude's. However hard we look, we can make out little more than a plump, freckled face (she is in the second row and the rest of her is hidden by the children in front). Glasses with thin black rims seem set into her face, suggesting she has deep-set eyes; hair is rough and frizzy, probably seldom brushed. I am particularly grateful therefore, in the light of this unrewarding picture, for the reports of the social worker responsible for Melanie at the time of the walk of October 17; and I feel these reports to be of more value than general comments forthcoming, which show unanimous dislike and distaste.

As this dossier builds up, I shall present the documents and 'reconstruction'; it need only be said at present that the failure to produce a picture and caption for a girl who was indeed on the expedition

8

and who played a major role in the calamitous events, is due to the fact that she was not among those reported missing to the police and press. She is Laurence Lelandes, daughter of the housekeeper at Forton Court (the home of Bess and Jane Plantain).

November 15, 1981

One

THE FOG HAD come suddenly, taking the lane with its ruts of mud still dry before winter, blotting the tree in the tricorne of grass where the lane forks left away from Mapperton, coming down on the girls walking there with the quick oblivion of a white childhood night.

Bess had been the first to see it coming. She was the only one of the girls taller than the hedges: she was taller, even, than Miss Stretherick, the Walks Woman, who had gone off to the right in search of blackberries. She stopped, crossed in a jump from the hollow-rooted tree where the road divided, peered over a barricade of nettle and dead rose.

' – I'm stuck!' A voice by the tree.

'Pull 'er out!'

'Snakes!'

The fields, the hills, the long shallows of grass and the trees still dark green gave off a gas, a white vapour, as if the whole scene, painstakingly constructed from matchsticks and strips of turf, had been placed in a bottle, clear as glass one minute, and the next, filled with smoke. Beaminster, church and market-place and square houses, stood out against the sky until the fog came up the streets and took it away. Now, this side of the town, the fields were bottomless and the dark trees a charcoal smudge.

The girls, still dawdling, gathered by a tree, a circle formed and broke: Nat, the dreamer, caught un-awares as always, in the middle. The twins leapt, Melanie heavily, unwillingly jumping with them, her spectacles falling, hair in an orange frizz against the fog. Jane, Bess's sister, drawn in against her will, danced a moment and pulled back. Class Four of St Jude's were coming up the lane. Already, without seeing over the hedge that shut them in a prison of straight lines and sky, they sensed that something had gone wrong with the walk.

' – Where's Miss? I want Miss!'
'C'mon! Yer didn't 'urt yerself!'

Some of the girls by the tree could read and others could not. The twins Mary and Mathilda, small eyes peering in thin faces, read out the placard on the tree. As they read, Nat stood accusing Melanie of pushing her under the hollow roots of the tree, of trying to kill her in this tree where, as the twins read aloud, villagers had collected at the time of the Great Plague to leave posies and say goodbye to their dead.
' – Snakes – and spiders,' said Nat.
' – The Posy Tree,' came the two voices above them. 'That's Ring a Roses. That's scary. You got a

12

ring o' spots – here, see? – an' you rubbed on the posy . . . '

Nat and Melanie fell to the hands of the twins, were hurled once more in a dance round the base of the tree. Class Four, distracted by a circle, broke into a run to join in. At six years old, few teeth between them, they bobbed like Hallowe'en pumpkins to the twins' stiff pumping.

'*Atishoo* – atishoo

Bess turned when the fog came up the hedge and seemed to wait there, although she knew that when it came over it would be sudden. She saw, in the impenetrable whiteness, the village on the flanks of the hills by Melplash where she lived with her parents; and she saw, in the same pricking out of characters in the smooth white, a stately vision of her school, Ferndale, porticoed, private, quite un-like the Melplash comprehensive where the twins' father taught or the village school, container of Melanie and Bess's younger sister Jane. The pillars and tennis courts vanished from the mind's eye, taken over by the white sightlessness of fog. Bess turned – too late – to call for the Walks Woman, to see what should be done now. By the Posy Tree, still clear, the girls leapt, laughing. 'Atishoo – atishoo – fall down dead!'

Bess ran where the lane forked right. The fog was coming up on the way the plague victims had been carried to a common grave below Beaminster. It wound round the trees, bringing the dank smell of

13

trees already smothered further down. Branches stood out, beckoned, before disappearing.

The Walks Woman's basket lay on the verge, ten feet in front of the advancing fog. A few small blackberries were in it and a stem of lords and ladies, a cluster of vermilion berries on a stout stalk. Now the last tree before the Posy Tree went into the shroud. By a low branch – it could be a nest of twigs – or, as the branch has already gone, it could be a head, walking away, Bess stops, picks up the basket and retreats, stepping backwards. She holds up the stem, as if the scarlet fruit could light the way out of the whiteness. The Walks Woman has gone, sucked down into the pestiferous air on the low road to Beaminster. Bess sees the placarded tree, vaguer now, and the leaping children.

'All fall down!'

Along the lane . . . she has been on the walk too, but apart . . a black-haired girl, almost as tall . . . but the hedge has been swallowed by now and there is nothing to measure her by. She is still fifty feet away . . . a girl with black hair in a black raincoat . . . already, the fog stands between her and the tree.

'Come on!' Bess breaks the band of children, the dancing ring. For the first time, they see the fog. Nat cries out. Bess leading, the twins behind with identical frowns, the small and less small in a straggling run . . . down on the lane where it breaks off to the left, away from the fog. On this lane, which will come out in a couple of miles to high ground, to the rim of an Iron Camp and open grass before it dips to the sea, the girls run, with the girl in the black raincoat always a few feet behind.

Two

ON THAT PART of the coast of Dorset, above Chesil Bank, there are green slopes, beyond them green hills like tilted hats, once terraced for vines or holding in the Roman soldier, and in them are lanes and byways that criss-cross and intersect in a labyrinth of contradictory lines. It wasn't surprising, therefore, that the helicopter pilot, Mr Jimmy Carr, sent out to rescue a boy from a cliff at West Bay and returning (it was a false alarm) empty-handed, mistook the group of girls for a returning school – tall Bess the leader – a school returning to the village of Kingston Russell, where, at that juncture in the lane, they did appear to be heading.

The pilot gazed down at Bess with some appreciation. Her long red-gold hair was fiery; redder than the few leaves already turning – chestnut, beech – in the forests that lay as part of the enigmatic shading on the board below him. He thought he'd come down and take a closer look. The girls would go out of sight sometimes, when there were trees on either side of the lane: for a few seconds he lost them altogether – until he saw a bunch of six-year-olds emerge on to a field, slipping and screaming in the mud. There had been cows along the lane, and the pilot wondered that the girls should have chosen this route back to Kingston Russell. He started to come down low. The hedges, to please him, lowered too at this point and he caught sight of a girl in a black coat, bringing up the rear. Then the red-haired girl again, and this made him come even lower: she was walking along with her head held high, and small white breasts clearly visible under a high, ruffled, transparent blouse. But then she lifted her head and looked up at him. She almost slipped. The mud was terrible.

Trying to recall the order of the procession, Mr Carr said two girls, with that immediate recognisable quality of twins, walked ahead of the black-haired girl, holding hands. The screaming six-year-olds were pulled back in from the field by a girl of eight or nine, bossy-looking. (When interviewed afterwards, the pilot said he couldn't remember for the life of him whether or not she wore glasses.) One girl was crying – extravagantly crying, and tugging at the sleeve of the red-haired girl of twelve or thirteen. He picked up distress. In the faces of the class of young ones he saw panic and fatigue. There was one small one – looked as if she were walking in her sleep – right up on the verge so that her ankle kept turning, and her head on one side. Only the girl in the black coat – and she must have been about twelve too, but one of those mysterious shut-in girls – seemed composed. It wasn't as if she knew where she was going to. It was more as if she were obeying some orders, going where she thought she had to go . . .

It wasn't, the pilot said, anything so much as the mixture of that girl's black, inward look, and the obvious agitation on the part of the others, that made him veer away for a fatal minute, rise a couple of hundred feet, and come face to face with the fog. He later admitted that he had not behaved with courage. But the white unexpectedness, the picture which, like Bess, he had been seeing in his mind's eye of the wooded hills down to Beaminster, the roofs of Melplash, the formed red brick of Parnham and the grey courtyard of Ferndale School, just going like that as if hit by a bomb of exploding vapour, caused him to rise even more steeply and go off towards the coast. By the time he'd circled, the girls had disappeared. There were other covered lanes, and he assured himself they had taken one, down to Kingston Russell. The fog wouldn't catch up with them. That was the strange thing: it seemed to have stopped, to hang like a white arras by that tree he'd often used as a guiding point – the tree with the words on a board, pinned to the bark.

And the sea is blue, as if summer had decided to lie late in the coves and shingle beds. Comforting, a blue quilt . . . the girls can come to no real harm. The pilot can't see them, as he makes his desultory search before flying down to Dorchester.

When the rushing sound goes, the girls take some time before they can be persuaded to go on down the lane. They can hear their hearts beating. With the roar and churning gone, they feel the absence of real birds. They see birds drowned in fog, like seagulls drowned in a sea that comes up suddenly to the top of the world. Only Melanie slipping on a beech nut and coming down hard breaks the quiet. 'Hey – Melanie – look at yer dress – what'll yer Mum say?'

The trees are high and growing all the time darker, the minds of the children are choked with the trees, which are so many they can't be counted, are too high to lean over to kiss goodnight, are as lost as the children, thrown down in a part of the map shaded evil. The fingers of the trees cling to the banks of fallen earth, rotting leaves, knuckles strain to open the oven door and push you in.

Lost. But lost is pushed out of the home, the step-mother pulls off her mother's mask, the wolf lets fall its grin. Leave me, says the mother, go away from me, I can't feed you, I don't want you, go out in the forest and drop your bread, but you will be the ones to be eaten.

In every child the dark knowledge of the mother grows, with the trees, blacker as they reach the sky, round fists of black twigs reaching up into the sky, black heads despising, turning away.

The forest is in me, says the mother. The wolf is in

me, to eat your bread and tear you to shreds. Go to the house with the roof of sugared almonds, look in the windows and nibble at the caramel shutters – see the dear old woman who will fatten you up behind bars. Go out in the world, you'll find it's not so sweet, my dears.

Lost. The children have nothing to scatter behind them. They stop – they turn – it can't be too late to go back.

They see the face of the witch behind them. She walks behind them but she leads. She knows where they're going – to their peril, to their end, in the sweet-gabled house in the trees.

The children run ahead, crying, screaming, in a lane so thickly wooded the fog hasn't yet crept into the kitchen, up to the oven door. They run under tall trees, fall in a tangle of roots, cling on to branches as sticky as rock. Laurie, the dark girl who appeared to them in their panic of Lost as the stepmother, the witch, the wicked dark one, is left behind once more, to walk alone in the path that will soon lead out on to hill.

Three

FIVE HOURS' HARD walking and they'd come to that long stretch of green, a second tier of protection against the sea, that goes up in a tall bank and bears the mark of early settlers – Romans, Saxons – who, like seabirds or a child passing with a trailing stick, have left their marks, half washed away. Bess stopped and looked out ahead. It seemed they were being pushed down the coast, for the fog, although it couldn't be seen to be moving, made any sort of circular return impossible. Already, apart from the panic stampede of Class Four, there had been difficulties. The twins, with their quiet, precise voice and air of self-assurance, had started the trouble.

'It's not a fog.'

'Nor a mist. It's not a mist.'

'What? What d'you mean?' Nat had run to catch up with them: she would believe anything. Melanie pushed her out of the way and she had to hobble behind, straining to overhear.

'It's nuclear war.' This was Mary, who had often proclaimed, in the games of hopscotch in Melplash playground, that she was twenty minutes older than her sister and must therefore jump first, know all.

'It said it was going to be today,' said Mathilda.
'On TV. It was on TV.'

'What's today?' Nat tried to overtake, ankles bending on the muddy bank.

'Nuclear war. That white stuff's the radiation.'

Melanie dropped back a second. She didn't remember anything on TV about today being the day for nuclear war but as soon as it was mentioned she saw the programme clearly. A man was talking, a white cloud went up against a vivid red sky. The cloud now spread from the palm-fringed island where it had begun and covered Melplash, particularly her home on the Whitehays Estate. She gave a giggle. On the TV she saw her Dad clutch his stomach as the poison fog came in. But of course her Dad could never have been on TV. She dropped another pace or two and waited for Jane to catch up.

'Your 'ome.' Jane was in earshot now and her small white face angled worriedly as Melanie spoke. Jane feared and hated Melanie. Her mother had said she had to stick out the village school until it was time to go to Ferndale, but she contrived 'flu and fractures so as to keep away. 'What about my h-h-home?'

Melanie slipped her arm through Jane's. Jane pulled away, but uselessly. Melanie's round brown eyes, snubby nose, freckles and fat cheeks settled down next to her. They were exactly the same height.

'It's been bombed. Your 'ome's been bombed.'

'What?' After the long walk, the frighteningness of the fog – being Bess's sister she knew when Bess was afraid and trying to conceal it – Jane felt a screech of terror rise in her throat.

'Yah. It was on TV.'

Jane stopped in her tracks. It was at this point that the helicopter pilot saw them – at first glance a docile group of girls, going back down to the village before the summer day went abruptly, letting a winter evening take its place.

Jane stood still. Forton Court, which stands above and slightly apart from Melplash: its roses on the long wall, the drawing-room that opens out on to the lawn . . . a woman in a blue dress carrying a basket of flowers . . . she heard her own voice, at its worst always when calling to her mother: 'M-M-Mummy!'

It was then that the plane came down low, the pilot saw Jane run to Bess, the tears, the bewildered looks on the faces of Class Four as they stumbled along in the rear. He really would have come down – he said so – if that dark girl hadn't seemed so completely sure of where she was going and what to do.

Jane was running, noisy sobs shaking out of her, as the pilot banked and turned away. 'It's the w-w-war.'

Bess shook off her sister's hand on her sleeve. Life was too kind to Jane at Forton Court. She got everything she wanted. The Princess and the Pea, Bess described her to her best friend at Ferndale.

'It was on T-TV!' Jane glowered up at Bess. Tears

began to escape. 'F-F-Forton Court got bombed – Melanie saw it!'

Bess shouted, but her rage was swallowed by the sound of the chopper's blades. And, she realised immediately, she should have been waving up for help, not listening to this nonsense from Jane.

'Melanie!' Now her voice could be heard. They were nearing the end of the bridle path under trees and the wide slope of sea, green banks and sky opened up to them. At the same time, as if to mock their journey, the sun turned and went off red behind a cloud – a shrinking sun, not waiting through a long evening as it had seemed to be going to do.

'What is all this about a war?'

Mary and Mathilda were quick to disclaim responsibility.

'Well it might be.' Mary nodded, spoke in states-man-like tones. 'This white substance. There is no reason to suppose it is simply fog.'

'It was odourless.' Mathilda added to the nodding. The twins had won scholarships to Ferndale and, being eleven, had arrived only a couple of terms back. Bess had seen them mostly in their white chemistry smocks, hurrying to the lab. In Melplash they were more rarely seen: their father, a maths master and widower, lived at Beaminster and taught at the comprehensive. But they came up sometimes, to play in the playground and visit Nat – her mother and their father were friends.

'Well, stop saying you saw it on TV then.' Bess was irritable, the vanishing of the sun had made long

23

shadows on the green slope. Is it better to stay under trees – but if it rains, it drips –

''Ow are we going to get home?' Melanie again, in a tone suggesting a trap question: if there's no nuclear war, then why can't we go home?

'The fog!' Bess turned again – no, it wouldn't be dry under the trees –

Nat's voice sounded from the slope. She had run out ahead, tired of the effort to understand. And there was what she wanted – just what she most liked. Rings, circles in the grass nibbled by sheep. Remains. History. She squatted, spilling the ammonite she always carried from her cardigan pocket. A part of the site had been excavated. A Roman temple shape. Nat's father had told her about these things.

Class Four heard her cry out. And Bess, not wanting to turn back to the trees, to brush against the girl in the black coat, went on. It wasn't so bad: in a dip; sheltered.

'Olden days.' Nat shouted, to encourage Class Four. But after their spurt to the temple site, weariness and fear took over and they fell, kicking, in the hollow walls of the temple sunk in the ground.

'This'll be a good place to dream.' Nat is encouraged by her mother to speak in this way. She won't help, though, with the settling down of Class Four. It is Bess, good-manneredly followed by the twins, who spreads duffles, says the fog will have lifted by morning, makes numb fingers dig for half-eaten Spangles packets that are stuck to coat linings. On the far edge of the site, the dark girl takes off her black coat and wraps herself in it, so as to make some pillow for her head. Bess feels the first spatter of rain – and at first she makes out she's invented them, these icy drops which have come so quickly from a sky that was blue and full of sun.

Four

STEADY, SENSIBLE BESS. She pulls over her thin blouse the white Shetland knit her mother made her last Christmas, scans the hillside and considers. If the rain gets worse . . . but it's hard to imagine moving Class Four, lying half knocked-out as they are in the grass, in the confines of the temple. The duffles will keep out a lot of the wet anyway. Bess knows she mustn't feel fear. And she knows her sister Jane has seen it in her already: together they saw their beds at home, Bess's room too tidy since she went away to Ferndale and lost sway, Jane's rose-patterned and crammed with babyish things. Both have seen their mother, worrying for them now: her worry will build to panic in them.

Coffee cups go down in a room devoted to country life, to the supremacy of the horse in oil and print, and chintz echoing the rush of green outside. Mrs

Plantain is with a friend. Bess lingers listening in the hall.

'Oh, she's the steady one. Bess is the one you can count on.' That laugh, the reaching for a Bittermint, the excited little giggle before the subject of the other one comes up. 'Jane is a real tomboy at the moment, of course. And they may get on better when she goes to the same school . . . but you know . . . she reminds me so much of Aunt Gertie . . . after all Aunt Gertie got what she wanted all her life . . . '

'What a magnificent house that was before they pulled it down.'

Bess has lost her power now she has gone to board-ing school. She can be counted on – when they see her – counted on to take away the coffee tray and hand it to the new housekeeper in the dark rooms at the back of Forton Court. She'll take Jane out on the pony, while Jane orders and screams. She is proud to be tall, with green eyes and the red-gold hair her father had loved to stroke (but he stopped suddenly, after her twelfth birthday). She is what her mother calls well-made.

At the foot of the hill, before it falls more quickly to the Fleet, and the bank of pebbles the sea made against itself that is Chesil Bank, and at a place where the sky touches the edge of the sea and the hill together in an early night cloud, a bluish Buddha shape lying along water and earth, Bess thinks she sees a car. It's a long way down, but what else can it be? There's a thin road there, she knows: the black thing is hardly a sheep pen, or a group of people. And as she looks down and the spots of rain hit her cheek and then die away again – as she brushes them her eyes are for a moment blurred – lights come on, hundreds of feet below. They must be car lights – what else? Bess rises, she doesn't look round to explain herself. She goes down the hill fast, only the top half of her in the fading light clearly visible, the white Shetland knit a flag as she goes.

No one does notice, at first.

'Who is she then?' A rare occasion: Mary is asking Mathilda a question. Their mouse-coloured heads are side by side, which is also rare for them. At home they lie top to tail, so that Mary's head looks out by Mathilda's ankles, and vice versa, like a child's stick drawings. But side by side is the best way to get covering from the coats, the second-hand gaber-dines their father had gone out dutifully and bought.

'She's *Laurie*.'

'Laurie?'

The dark girl has begun to intrigue the twins. She lies apart, and seems to have taken a small white book from her pocket. Melanie has gone up to her once and come back looking baffled, an unlikely expression for Melanie. Mathilda, self-important, stretches out under the gaberdines. Three inches of rainwear slip away from Mary's outer leg.

'Dad has her for maths 'n history. She's French.'

'*French?*' Mary jerks the navy blue over her, Mathilda is pulled in as if on a string.

'Well, her mother's French anyway. She was never married. She oughtn't to say she's Mrs, that's what Dad says. Laurie's Dad is French but she's never seen him once.'

Silence. The twins' four roundish eyes gaze over the coats' rim at the phenomenon.

'Poor thing.'

'I don't think she ever speaks . . . that's what someone told our Dad, anyway.'

Melanie, breaking off from talking posh with Jane – and this talk was the greatest agony to Jane – heard the twins, rolled over in the trench and reflected. She moved to one side and pulled a book from her coat pocket. The book had the words *Nature Diary* on the cover and a picture of a red squirrel, never actually spotted on any of the walks. Walks Woman had given this diary to Melanie but Melanie has not used it for Nature Notes. She folds back the cover, lifts a green felt-tip from its crack between My Diry Privit Keep Out and the margin of the facing page, and begins to write.

My ist day runing away from hom and a big fog com down an everyon runing the same way. Mary and Mattillda says it is war and newklear bom I hope my dad is bomed and my mum too there is a girl here she is Lorri and she has a white book an I says what is the book and she says it is a missle. I seen missles on TV and Lorri has one now and they are for killing Rushans and she got

28

black hair like my doll Sara. Bess is bossy I dont like her and she is posh and Jane is posh I like Lorri.

Beauty and the Beast. In the long, rambling house where Laurie lives – in the part at the back where she lives in the dark rooms like a flower snapped off its stalk – in the passages that lead on the upper floors to rooms with fat beds and pillows fattened every night for the rich to lie on – in the cupboard where the children hide, playing the game that makes your heart thump, the hide in the early hours of a delphinium blue afternoon, the seek as it spills over to evening time, to anger, confusion, guilt. Here, Melanie, the beast, has seen Laurie and has lowered her eyes in love.

Only once or twice, but it's worth waiting a life-time. Melanie of the mangy pelt, small beast eyes deep in a head sloping back, stupid, sad. She lies in the cupboard, waiting for the magic kiss that will free her of her bestial curse and bring her handsome legs, a beautiful boy's face like at the pantomime.

But Beauty goes past without looking.

Or, she stands in the cupboard, in the sheets and scalloped linen towels, with a man's arms round her, in the dark.

Now, Bess, what do you have to do?

Bess speaks aloud to give herself strength, but it's

worse than keeping silent in the long zigzagging run down the hill to the road. Her voice hits the edge of the Land Rover, parked there and empty, headlights so strong that if they turned and blinked at her she knew she would smash to pieces, shatter down the side of the road to the sea. They won't, of course – unless –

'Hullo!' If there's anyone there they'll hear her now. Silence. Bess imagines lovers going down to the sea, falling together on pebbles, rolling into foam from the rump of stones left by high tide. Or murder – a sack – kittens crouched and hopeless in a sack – silence.

This silence is like the fog. It enters your lungs, it takes away question and quick response. It leaves silence. Bess feels her throat go into one of the spasms that irritate her mother at home, the dry coughing, ticklish, raspish, that makes her mother say, 'Bess, for God's sake go and get a glass of water!'

And the sky. It joins the silence, in mute agreement: it loops in a wash of Indian ink a night pictography. The blue Buddha lies sideways, feet sticking up out of the sea. Camels, flamingoes in the last rays of the sun setting red, the caravansarai of night crosses the sky. Bess is still coughing. The silence has to end. The spasm in the throat has to be punctured, by sound.

High on the hill, in the circle of worship the Romans left and which no one has been able to decipher, Nat half-dreams with her eyes open to the stars. In this state she can summon her father from a book (for he wrote books on stones and ancient places) and she sees him rise from a book bound in the wide dark blue leather of the sea. He stands on Chesil Bank pointing outward. That's where he has gone. She must follow him. He is in the Atlantic, which brings in silver ingots and porcelain with mossy barnacles from Portugal and once, in the eighteenth century, he told her, a merman thirteen feet long. She must go after him because she has waited long enough now and she knows he won't be washed up there, part of the haul drawn in invisible threads to land in the great net of Chesil Bank. She used to make her mother take her once a week – to see if he was there, eyes closed, lying on the stones. But in the end her mother wouldn't go.

'But he is over the – in the Atlantic, isn't he?'

How tired her sigh, her kick to kick the door of the wood stove shut.

'Yes. But you won't find him there Nat please – '

The sound of the horn brings Nat tumbling down the hill. Once – twice – three times it sounds. Even Class Four wake, move drowsily down the hill, a pale centipede in the last light. Melanie and Jane are ahead – older than Nat – you couldn't tell they're not inseparable. Nat runs to catch up. She doesn't want the twins, the grudging, narrow shoulders, obstinate lips clamped like when they have to follow their father on a friendly visit to her mother's front room. Nat doesn't want him, the smell of his pipe, his jolly voice greeting Nat's mother as if he had just come across her by accident in a country lane.

So clear out to sea. The sound has broken Bess's cough. She could suck in the clear air like lemonade in a straw. But she has seen the fog, coming down on them over the hill. It must have covered Kingston Russell by now. At first she thought the fog was night – it was like the underbelly of a great bird, downy wings folded, owl's eye for the half-moon lying aslant. But it was fog. Or is it really the bomb – if it's the bomb, are there people stranded there already like dying rabbits – eyes staring out of eaten-away faces? Bess knows that men like to kill – like when Mr Plantain stands and fires – and the shot goes faster than a whispered sigh on a telegraph wire – and a Chinese bird, so proud and gold and green, falls like a sack of rubbish at his feet.

Nat catches up with Jane and Melanie.
    'Can I come with you?'
    'Oh all right,' says Melanie.

Now it is dark. Class Four are pushed on to the floor of the Land Rover and Nat, Melanie and Jane climb in to the seats.

The twins come down last, a few paces behind Laurie. The headlights pick them out. Disney jungle eyes in the blackness, as the jerky identical figures march down over the crest of the hill.

Five

WE MUST TAKE advantage of the dark, in which Bess, who's had a couple of driving lessons from her father, steers the Land Rover on the coast road to Weymouth. As the screen goes blank, we leave for the moment the 'imaginative reconstruction' of these days in the girls' exile from their homes – days in the calendar of nightmare, which will end with the appalling events we are now attempting to understand. These services will be called on again; for the moment it is most useful to examine the case histories, compiled by sociologists, teachers and psychiatrists, of these girls and young women. (There are also two fragments of a journal kept by Laurence Lelandes.) Thus, perhaps, will the psychopathology of the developing female be more fully comprehended; as also the mythology sustaining our concept of the feminine in society.

Case History I   Bess Plantain

FATHER: Ralph Plantain, businessman. Private means. Owner of Forton Court Estate.

Business: small factory in Taunton manufacturing riding crops, saddles, etc. Keen sportsman and rider to hounds. In 1975 suffered a major hunting accident with the Melplash Hunt and was hospitalised for six months. No longer an active sportsman; has diversified business interests, to include aqualung and wind-surfing equipment.

MOTHER: Mary Plantain. Refused on all occasions to give interviews, even at the time of her daughter's first bout of nervous coughing. Known to be obsessive on the subject of cleanliness, and to suffer from 'housewife's psychosis'. Not close to either of her daughters, but it has been observed that male characteristics in the younger daughter Jane (climbing trees, 'tomboy' behaviour, etc.) are seen with disapproval. Non-smoker. Fastidious. In 1975 developed lumbago. In the last year (1981) found she was no longer able to continue with household chores, despite daily help from the village, and employed Mrs Strang as housekeeper. Since the arrival of Mrs Strang, reports show an increased fastidiousness on the part of Mrs Plantain, thus no doubt leading to increased tension in the home.

Report by Dr Ross, Freudian Psycho-Analyst, aged 76. He is retired, resident at Taunton and a close friend of Dr Cottle, family doctor to the Plantains:

At the time of our first interview Bess was twelve years of age. She had just begun her first term at a boarding school, Ferndale, when the attacks of nervous coughing began to afflict her, and her G.P., Dr Cottle of Melplash, decided to send her to me; apart from a natural shyness at seeing a member of the medical profession, and a certain anxiety regarding her future career at the school, she gave the impression of a well-balanced personality, quiet but not retiring; intelligent, observant and possibly stubborn.

It did not appear difficult at first to ascertain the cause of Bess's nervous symptoms.

Her family circle consisted of her father, a man of unusual charm and the possessor of a forceful character, who had been injured in a hunting accident when Bess was five years old and who had since spent a disproportionate amount of his time at home, going out to supervise his business only two days a week. Bess had been his special favourite of the two daughters. While she attended the village school and was home by four o'clock and at the week-ends, Bess's father invented games for them both to play, built toys, slides, swings, chutes, etc. for her to enjoy and generally forgot his semi-

invalid state in her presence. They wrote and illus-
trated books together – Bess brought a sample to
her first interview. The father was clearly talented
on many fronts and the owner of an original mind:
the book was charming, though Bess showed a
distinct ambivalence to it (this of course could be
attributed to a rejection of 'babyish' material on
reaching the stage of embarkation on a new school
career).

Bess's mother was the exact opposite of her husband. Where he was kind, encouraging and able to
enter without difficulty into the imaginative world
of a child, the mother showed distinct coldness to
children in general, and in particular to Bess. Jealousy
clearly played a part here; and it was perhaps partly
because Bess was such a favourite of her husband
that Jane the younger daughter was seen as a dis-
appointment by the wife. In the younger daughter
(the parents had hoped for a son) the mother found
'tomboyish' characteristics; and both appearance
and behaviour were exactly opposed to those of
Bess, who gave the impression of being a 'quick
developer' in both the physical and the cerebral
sense. From her own remarks on the first interview,
Bess would have been happy if her mother had
vanished from her life altogether. But had this come
about, she would have found herself a virtual
orphan. For, shortly after her twelfth birthday in
March 1980, Bess's father turned away from her –
spurned would not be too strong a word – and the

close relationship abruptly ceased. Bess's migraines developed shortly after, to be followed in the summer, her last term at the village school, by an attack of nervous coughing resulting in total voice loss for a duration of nine days.

It is not my practice to inform patients still ignorant of sexual matters with facts they are not yet ready to digest. However, it seemed even in our first sessions that Bess was trying to convey the sense of lack of love between her parents and the subsequent effect of the burden of her father's affections on her shoulders, at least until her twelfth birthday. I asked her, therefore, if her mother and father shared a bedroom and to this Bess replied 'No'. She added that on Christmas mornings, when she and her sister opened their presents, her father came and sat on her mother's bed. Otherwise, they had separate rooms, not only at opposite ends of the house, which is a substantial one, but on different floors also. The next remark Bess made seemed to me highly significant. 'He dresses up on Christmas morning. It's the best part of the day.' When asked what she meant, she replied that her father, when the presents were opened, went to a cupboard in the passage and took out the 'pink': hunting coat, cap and riding crop: in short, the regalia he was no longer physically able to don in the field. 'Then he sits on the end of the bed, dressed like he used to be, and we all play with the toys.'

It does not seem an improbable conjecture, that Bess's father, his lost virility represented by the riding crop, was seen by his daughter to be a 'normal' husband (i.e. a husband sharing his wife's bed, 'active in the field') only once a year on Christmas mornings, and this in make-believe. His possible impotence as a result of the accident must thus have been suspected by her on one level, at least.

It should be possible to adduce that Bess, ignored by her mother and adored by her father, then ignored by her father after her twelfth birthday, was clearly in love with and violently upset by her father. Loss of voice resulting from attacks of *tussa nervosa* would not be unexpected after a volte-face of this nature. It would be unlikely that a child of this age would understand the sexual embarrassment felt by many men on the occasion of the reaching of pubertal age of their daughters. She would feel, simply, rejection; and it could be said that the combination of this rejection with a new school career might well produce symptoms of a more severe nature in a less well-balanced personality. (The loss of voice, incidentally, I see as an unconscious imitation of the father's lack of sexual potency, which is also equated in the child's mind with the hunting cry, a loudness of voice, in the field.)

So we might feel some confidence in putting forward the view that Bess's rejection by her father was the prime cause of the nervous symptoms.

It was only after several sessions that a further factor began to emerge. This was another relationship, not at first alluded to, with the mother's younger stepbrother, who was known in the household as 'Uncle' although in fact no blood tie existed between himself and the child. It transpired that 'Uncle' had one afternoon in the summer holidays of 1979, when Bess was eleven years of age, followed her where she was playing, 'sliding on bales', and pinned her down, leaning against her so hard that she was unable to struggle to her feet. As 'Uncle' was clearly an attractive young man, and maturity has in the last decade tended to set in as early as ten or eleven years of age, I asked Bess if she had enjoyed the experience. She said she definitely had not. Her first thought, apparently, had been that she should call her father, and get him to give the young man a good thrashing with his riding crop.

Dr Ross's subsequent additions to the Clinical Report on Bess Plantain before the walk of Saturday October 17th are in the process of transcription. Other dossiers will follow, as will Bess's extended Clinical Report. At present, as a wisp of fog blows across our screen – maybe it's the white vapour of the coastal hills, maybe smoke from the projectionist's cigarette – we find ourselves back by the sea, but this time under tall trees, suspiciously like coconut palms.

Six

Bright sun. A clear blue sky over the coast. A tangle of creepers and tropical trees in the gardens where the girls spent the night – and an abandoned Land Rover, which got as far as the Sub-Tropical Gardens and Swannery beyond Abbotsbury before the petrol ran out. (Was this why the owners had left it on the road? To go for petrol? But why hadn't they gone on until the tank emptied? We will never know.) A kiosk. The girls have aching legs after the night out. But their step quickens. The kiosk stands like a chalet in a picture postcard. It's closed.

'Sunday morning,' says Mary. 'It wouldn't be open anyway.'

'I want to go to the Swannery,' says Nat. She pronounces it Flannery. 'Let's go. Please.'

'I think we could get in through the side door,' says Mathilda. 'It looks as if the padlock hasn't closed.'

Class Four is beginning to catch up with the others. Bleary eyes, dribbly noses, they don't see the blue calm of the water coming up on Chesil Bank, the blue sky that looks as if you could hit your head on it. They see, or rather sense, a kiosk's bounty: choc bars, Mr Whippy, sandwiches with tomato and without tomato, with ham. Crisps, salt 'n vinegar. Maybe even pork scratchings. There's Mathilda already, triumphant at the kiosk's side door. Coca-Cola, Fanta. Mars and Crunchie: eyes as round as Maltesers, Class Four struggle up the patchy-grassed incline to the hut.

It had been a difficult night. The Sub-Tropical Gardens, laid down two hundred years ago in a geological fault in the coast hill, have trees and shrubs out-rageous in size and lushness: there are bananas, even: if this willow-pattern, or exotic eighteenth-century backdrop can thrive here, it seems to suggest, why has England decided to remain so northern in its appearance and vegetation? Is this corner of colonial memory not proof of unlimited possibility? Cer-tainly, Bess can remember a visit with her father when she was small, and Mr Plantain looking up at the great height of palms and laughing and mock-shuddering at the whole thing. 'So monotonous. No seasons. Not the life for me.'

'Aunt Gertie made a success of India,' Mrs Plan-tain said.

But Mr Plantain's attention had been drawn to a strange tree, which bore the legend, on a cedarwood plaque, of its ability to shoot into flower once in every hundred years. The flower was blue: its sud-den shooting into an eerie, pointless life marked the end of the life of the tree. Mr Plantain had stood

41

pondering this. 'I'll be dead by the time it flowers,' he announced with some resentment, as if trying to guess how to break the cycle of the strange flowering, as if forcing it to break forth more often would in some way prolong his own life.

Bess had decided on bedding down the girls in the long greenhouses. But the floors were hard and the outline of cacti, and tropical plants with fleshy cheeks, terrifying. 'They can.' Nat had a store of information; she was telling Jane. 'The big man-eating lilies. That's one over there. They just open their mouths. And you're sucked in.'

'Don't be silly.' Jane the tomboy felt for the penknife she kept in her pocket, all the same. 'It's flies they eat. Flies.'

'They practise on flies.'

The dark girl was apart as usual, and had refused to come into the greenhouse, giving a curt shake of the head when Jane had been sent out to find her. Wrapped in her coat, she had lain on a bank of spongy moss under a tree with long creepers that came down like braids of black hair to the ground. Her white book with its ivory cover shone palely in the light from a half-moon that was pinned like a spangled slide to the braids of the top of the tree.

'She's a Roman Catholic.' Melanie had taken advantage of Bess's discomposure to crawl the length of the greenhouse floor.

'How d'you know?' Bess looked down on Melanie from a lofty height. She had let her hair down now, and even in the pale darkness it shone gold, the real thing. Melanie felt blinded, she wanted to climb it, to be pulled into the chamber of Bess's inner eye.

'She tole me.' This was a lie; Melanie had overheard the twins. But Bess nodded, as if satisfied. She glanced out at the solitary figure under the tree.

'Yes. She is Catholic. She's got a missal.'

Melanie gazed up, anxious.

'What she goin' to do with it, then?'

Bess laughed. 'Anything she wants, I suppose.'

Melanie stares, more awestruck than ever, at the beautiful dark girl she loves.

But they've hardly embarked yet, on this journey where Melanie will use her skills to so great an advantage, at first anyway. They are still in the improbable forest, where even Mary and Mathilda think they see a gingerbread house, and pieces of bread left in an orderly pattern on the ground and Class Four dreams of a basket, covered always with a white cloth, hiding cookies with raisins inside, and a loping wolf on the edge of the path.

Nat is the only one not afraid, in this landscape of half-dream, a landscape she is used to inhabiting. When morning light comes through the palms, she is the first to wake. Later she rises, she follows the others in the pantomime glow, to the little hut by the edge of the sea. Where the counter is made of white icing, and there are marzipan chairs.

The voices of Class Four are shrill.

'I want that one.'

'I want it.'

'I want exactly the same.'

Crunchies are pounded into pockets, Kit Kats dismembered, the hiss and spurt of Coke cans make a miniature air-raid in the hut. The kiosk sells sneakers, and these are jammed on to feet, laces knotting and snarling in clumsy fingers.

'I want blue sneakers.'

'I want the blue ones.'

'Red is my favourite.'

The sandwiches are old and stale-looking. But Bess fills a carrier with them, and with despised bottles of ginger beer. And with toffees, the dull-looking sort which have also been rejected by the girls. For, in crossing the shingle strip between the beach and the Gardens, she has seen the fog again, coming up behind them so that soon only the sea will be clear, under that blue sky that looks as if it could never be contaminated. The fog comes up vague, bear-shaped, with a small head against the still-clear sky and a polar, shaggy stomach devouring the hills where the girls had walked and driven in the car.

Not that it's the first time Bess has seen the fog since settling in the gardens for the night. She saw it falling like white petals on the great tree which sheltered Laurie. The black braids whitened, Laurie seemed to lie there unperturbed at the blanket that

44

might soon come down and stifle her as she lay. She still held the prayer book. Why didn't she care?

Seven

LIKE CLUES THAT drop suddenly into the unconscious mind, solving the mosaic of childhood, the patterns of loves and hates that are laid down in a game without rules, three visitors have come to show themselves to the girls, to guide them on the next stages of their journey. They are: the car, which gave Bess, at the wheel, the sense of mastery so long gone; the padlock on the door of the hut, which like a key in a dream needed only a slight twist to open; and the boat, which Bess sees now, beached on the shingle, and tilting to the side in its bed of stones. The boat isn't big – but it's big enough, of course, to take them out of the fog – out to sea – not too far but far enough into the tempting blue horizon. And the fog, politely whiter than ever it was on the hill – so white it might be the giant crest of a wave, or the wingspan of a monstrous gull – is moving in fast. The lianas, the palms, the ridge at the top of the greenhouses in the Sub-Tropical Gardens have disappeared. Behind the hut the fog hangs, accommodating itself to the harsh strictures of the sea.

In the kiosk, Jane is the first to see the blankness from the small rear window. But Nat is the one who has found that the hut contains a secret, and she cries out. A room, a tiny room but still a room, that leads out of the partitioned-off bit, where the tea lady fills the urns. Nat signals to Jane.

'Come on here, Jane!'

It's true, there is a low door: the room is made of wood, it must jut out, invisible from the exterior because of the cliff overhang, into the rock. There is a small window. The white rock it looks on to is as blank to the gaze as the fog that makes a wall at the back of the hut.

'I want to live here.'

Nat is proprietorial already. She shuts the door, which is stained planks nailed together. It's dark in here, with a pitch-pine smell. There's a bed – that's the strange thing – pushed up against the window, an ordinary single bed. Next to it is a camp bed. Both have messy blankets and duvets. Otherwise, there is fishing tackle, and pots of glue and a broom. 'We can play housey,' Nat says.

Jane goes straight to the single bed. She lies down on it. It's lumpy and the smell this time is very unpleasant indeed – like rotting fish wrapped in newspaper.

'I want that one,' Nat says.

Outside, Bess is running up the beach from the boat with the strides of a running dream. The shingle pushes her gently back, the corners of the hut ahead of her begin to go in fog, like paper burning to ash. 'Out,' she calls – but the waves, and the fog that's clamping down now over the cliff, swallow the sound. 'Out!' All she can see, leaning against the wall of the kiosk, is the dim shape of Laurie, in the black raincoat with the collar turned up. And the voices of the children squabbling are still there: 'I'll have this one.'

Jane is drawn suddenly to the camp bed. It's small, it suits her. To Nat's surprise she gives up the bigger bed at once, goes to lie on the impermanent, rickety bed. She puts her thumb in her mouth.

Nonplussed, Nat climbs into the grown-up bed, with its smell and its snug position up against the wall. She looks eagerly at Jane, for the game to continue. But Jane's eyes are tight shut and her thumb right up in her mouth as if it would disappear for ever.

The house in the clearing, the beds, the porridge bowls. Jane won't sleep yet in the biggest bed, the bed with the smell of Father Bear and the frilly nightdress poking out under the pillow. She's not the size for the little bed either, and the spoons shrink in her hand when she picks them up.

There are no trees hiding this hut, but it is a lost hut too, walled in by fog and sea, a hut where you can't find your name and the clock ticks loudly, telling you the lies your mother's mother told her and now

47

it's telling you. The tiny chair grips your haunches when you sit down. In the vagueness of the fog, you wander to the table, a sudden giant, and open a newspaper that must be Father Bear's, next to a napkin ring he folds his family into after every meal. You try to speak.

Freedom, namelessness, in the white fog. Jane eats the porridge, climbs into the big chair, crunches the baby furniture under foot.

A picture hangs on the wall. A tower, encircled by brambles, a single window at the top and inside a young prince, asleep. It's for you to walk there, says the clock. The prince lies with an arm trailing the floor, in his dead sleep from which only the walking, fighting Jane will bring him back.

Noises outside. The bears bring with them the snap and crackle of forest twigs, of conversations over-heard, of catching out the child in its wicked act. Jane tries to speak, to call out. But her voice is both high and low, and it clashes together in her throat. They open the door and the fog swirls in.

'Who's been sleeping in my bed?' says Mother Bear, for it is true, Jane lay there longest, with her head on the nightdress that smells of fur, milk and scent.

Class Four are huddled on the plank floor of the kiosk. Chocolate and snot run in channels from nose to mouth. In some cases, the new brightly-coloured sneakers have been done up in preparation for a three-legged race: the left-hand shoe tied to the right-hand shoe of the neighbour, and so on. They rise with difficulty, in reply to Bess's shrill call.

The twins are playing chess on their miniature chess set at a table by the tea-urn laid for tea. They look up as soon as Bess comes in, pull out the tiny pawns on their pins and snap the box shut. They seem to understand more quickly and respectfully than other children. They march up to Bess. She says: 'There's a boat. On the beach. We'll take everything we can.'

Mary and Mathilda follow her glance. They move mechanically, gracefully through the mess of Class Four. There are cartons, which they fill with crisps and drinks and what's left of the chocolate. They stagger out into the whiteness, and vanish from sight.

Melanie is helping herself to the contents of the souvenir case. Bess begins to speak, then holds back.

It's just a question of honesty. But Bess has no one to say this to. At Ferndale, where she fitted in so easily, Miss Knowles the History Mistress would have helped her in this, the eternal question for children on the edge of maturity: what is dishonest, and what is permissible? In extreme circumstances, that is.

But did Melanie even know the circumstances were extreme? It was unlikely. Simply – a foggy Sunday morning on a walk that had got out of control . . . So, having smashed the glass case that stood, with a wooden counter on top of it, in the centre of the kiosk – did she think she had committed a crime? No. Did she have the right to stuff a carrier bag with seaside souvenirs, printed scarves and the like? No, of course she didn't. For her, these things, by being in a glass case, belonged to a different category from, say, the sneakers, which appeared, in their loose jumble, to belong to humanity.

This, however, would be nothing if Bess hadn't seen that Melanie had the cash register too – on the floor, there – she must have pulled it down and forced open the tray.

And now the money is going into the carrier bag along with the souvenirs and a paperweight with white flakes inside that snow on a field of rabbits if you hold it upside down.

'Melanie!'

The money scatters. Melanie looks up. The panic is on now, Class Four is stampeding to the door, someone slips on a half-eaten Cornetto. A scream. And it's when they're halfway down, over the pebble banks to the sea, that Bess sees they're lacking Jane and Nat. The twins are helpful, they return for them. Thoughtful, too, for when they manage to wake Jane from her infant's sleep and to drum sense into the ever-dreaming Nat, they remember to bring the bedding down: the stinking eiderdown and a duvet and even a large tarpaulin they find in a corner of the hidden room. Bess understands, as the twins stagger down to the beach with their load, that they know too just how frightening the situation has become. They won't be home tonight. She tries to thank them. But the four, smallish brown eyes are dull to the rest of the world, they light up only when they are together and alone.

Now the boat goes out to sea. If the pilot who had been so nearly their saviour on the hills above Abbotsbury had thought to come back at this moment, he would have seen a strange sight, reminiscent more, perhaps, of pictures of fleeing refugees than of a comic artist, such as Lear. It was probably the presence of the pale, dark girl in the prow of the boat that gave this sense of desperation, of escape: she'd pulled her black coat over her head, giving at a distance the impression of a crouching nun. Otherwise, the blobby faces of Class Four, the dreamy features of Nat and the angular, rather quick-lined appearance of Jane would certainly have returned him in memory to those drawings of the Jumblies seen in childhood and not forgotten: in a sieve they went to sea.

The sea may be cold, but it's blue. The sun has ownership of the sea, while land has gone entirely now, given over to fog. The children peer out at the horizon, there's nowhere else to look.

Except for Melanie, that is, whose head is deep in her carrier bag. When she pulls her head out, her hand dives in. She is counting her money.

Bess and Jane are both efficient at the oars. Mr

Plantain taught them, on a lake in Scotland where they once went for their holidays.

Laurie, still as a ship's figurehead carved in wood, sits in the prow and stares out. She bisects the square of sea, the shingle bank the sea has thrown up against itself and the parallel line of the Fleet, the blue rule of sea beyond the Bank.

It is Nat who first sees land. She points and calls. It may be true – or, like stories made up for children, it may not be true. It seems, over the short, stubby waves with a gleam of foam, that rocks are sticking up out of the sea. It's a long way off, but Bess smiles in sudden relief. Melanie still scrabbles in her bag, pulling out this time a ladies' compact and a rolled-gold lighter, with Weymouth Sands written in fancy lettering across its front. The gold and the mirror in the compact catch the sun, and for a moment everyone is dazzled, as if a new sun had popped up out of the sea. The light gives Bess a headache, like the beginning of one of her migraines. She loses her temper, which she can do very violently.

'Shut up, Melanie! For God's sake, put those back!'

Melanie, from the floor of the boat, looks up. A crafty smile makes lopsided that doughy face, slab cheeks and freckled nose. The brown eyes go bright. 'O.K., Bess.'

Case History II   Melanie Ayres

Report by Social Worker Ms S. B. Potts, of Bridport, Dorset:

Melanie Ayres has twice been placed with foster parents, on the last occasion in June 1979. On February 1st 1981 she returned to her home in Whitehays Estate. It was ruled that her parents Tommy and Denise Ayres resume responsibility for Melanie at their home at Whitehays, the Melplash council estate, but should thereafter receive regular visits from a social worker. Melanie had been a 'battered baby' at the age of nine months and allegations of the brutality of the father, Tommy Ayres, continue to be made at Whitehays. Denise Ayres was herself in a battered women's refuge in Taunton, until the closing down of the home on health grounds by the Council. Her own experiences at the hands of her husband, an unemployed farm labourer, had led her to acts of brutality against Melanie: on several occasions a cut, bruise or graze was suspected by Dr Cottle of having been perpetrated by the mother. Melanie had always appeared attached to her mother, however, while demonstrating considerable hostility to her father; and it was only on the occasion of having to terminate the fostering situation in Bridport that Melanie showed her feelings for her real mother to have substantially cooled, and those for the foster mother to have heightened considerably.

Recent visits on the regular basis proposed have shown worrying traits developing in Melanie, not the least of which are compulsive story telling and mild kleptomania. At the shop–cum–post–office in Melplash, Mrs Biggs reported continual petty pilfering by Melanie, who was always 'caught at it', seemed to wish to be detected, and invariably apologised and replaced the article. Mrs Biggs, having frequently complained to Mrs Ayres and having said on the most recent occasion that she would prosecute, came to us in the last resort. At my request, she has agreed to give Melanie one more chance.

In the case of the compulsive lying, it appeared both to my colleague Mr Davison and myself that Melanie was more interested in saying what she knew to be the opposite of the truth, than in the possible consequences of so doing. She told us individually, for instance, that (a) she had taken a school library book of some value, missing for several weeks, to an outlying field and buried it 'just for fun', and (b) that she had sold the book to a girl in Bridport, whose 'dad was rolling'. On investigation, neither proved to be true: certainly Melanie had brought the book home, which was against the rules, but Mrs Ayres on the occasion of the visit of the Mobile Library to the village, had handed it back and it had been accepted without the assistant noticing its true home. Melanie, on being taxed with this and other discrepancies in her stories, replies invariably that she can't remember what she has said. As this is clearly not the truth either, Mr Davison and I decided against referring Melanie for psychiatric treatment on the grounds of amnesia, kleptomania, etc. (this might cause further rebellious acts) and to continue with regular visits and surveillance.

In September 1981, however, eight months after her return to Whitehays, other symptoms of Melanie's disturbed state (or so we are told by those who believe in psychic phenomena) began to manifest themselves. Mrs Ayres was the first to report the throwing about of plates, cups and so on; neighbours on the estate complained that the sound of heavy furniture being shifted loudly and energetically kept them awake at night. The obvious answer, that the house is lived in by a violent man with a history of battering, has not satisfied some of the Melplash residents. Instead, undesirable publicity was focussed on Melanie by an anonymous call, from the village, to the local newspaper, the *Bridport Advertiser*. Reporters and photographers came, and Melanie was front page news as the progenitor of a poltergeist. On the occasion of my call, the Bishop had already paid his visit and Mrs Ayres announced with satisfaction that the house was now quiet. It was true, Melanie seemed extremely subdued and also there were no external signs of violent treatment from her father or mother. I recommended that the whole 'poltergeist' episode should be forgotten as soon as possible – Melanie was over-dramatising herself, and the incidents led her into even vaguer areas between truth and lies – but this has not to date been possible. Shortly after the exorcism, disturbances started up again. Three outbreaks of flying objects, mattresses soaked in water and curtains wrenched from their pelmets, have been recorded at the Ayres home on the Whitehays Estate. The most recent, taking place three weeks before the walk of Saturday October 17th, concerned Mr Ayres, who was admitted to Taunton Hospital with a fractured foot. It appeared that the dresser, an old heavy country piece, had 'moved forward' in the kitchen and crushed him against the wall. Melanie, who came in half an hour later from the playground (and she had been seen there by several children) disclaimed all responsibility for this. No trick mechanism was discovered under or behind the dresser that could have activated it on the arrival in the kitchen of Mr Ayres.

Report by the Bishop of Taunton on the Ayres Case, Whitehays, Melplash:

Asked to give a few words on the haunting of the Ayres home, I must stress that I speak casually and confidentially: none of the family is known to me, and I am informed by the vicar, the Rev. J. Lee, that not one member has ever visited the church or sought advice from him. Thus, I give my impressions only, to assist in this difficult case.

Melanie Ayres, before the exorcism ceremony, was a very highly-strung young girl: tense and clearly badly frightened. An element of publicity-seeking which I have come to look for in some of these cases was markedly absent, and when she could find her voice at all it was to beg me for some assurance that the 'horrible thing' would go away. I tried to reassure her, although it is not so easy, of course, to rid a particularly persistent psychic phenomenon of its habits. Melanie Ayres told me that 'it' gave her instructions, always to do something naughty – and when it wasn't causing objects to fly through the air, it was telling her to do such things as steal and bury library books, empty out all the salt in the salt cellar, etc. She said she thought her father might have sent it to her as a punishment. I refrained from going too deeply into this, and suggested to Melanie that she should be confirmed in the church, which would very likely put an end to all manifestations. To date, she has refused with such vehemence that one can only suspect the presence of a counterforce, unknown to her, of course, which has lodged itself within.

I fear this will be a hard case. In view of the events succeeding the walk of Saturday October 17th, I have appealed to the Archbishop of Canterbury for further rites of exorcism to be permitted at Whitehays Estate.

Eight

'Look!'
'Watch out!'
'Let me out!'
'It's your fault I got my feet wet. Now my feet are wet.'
'Oh, get out of the way.'

A small cove, the stones on the beach are Brob-dingnagian, each pebble the size of a plate.
'Ow! I can't walk on this!'
'My feet hurt!'

Bess leaves the boat last. It's true, the large, round stones are very hard to walk on. And for the first time, her eyes fill with tears. What is this hard, desolate, stony place, no part of her soft Dorset childhood? A piece of land like a stone wall, ragged, dangerous, sticking out into the sea.
'We're on an island.' Nat cries out with pleasure.
'Treasure Island.' Class Four crowd round her.
'Swiss Family Robinson.' Jane saw the film last Christmas. Her mother had laughed when she said she'd like to be the mother, Mrs Robinson. 'You're not that type, Jane. You're the adventuring type!' But Jane wanted to be Mrs Robinson.

'Coral Island.'

Mary and Mathilda exchange glances.
  'We're not – '
  'On an island.'

Class Four pay no attention.
  'Pirates.'
  'That man with the funny hand.'

Melanie struggles over the giant pebbles with her heavy carrier bag. She is scowling: even from the back she is a menacing, unattractive sight.

Bess is the one who calls out at the stupid excitement of Nat and Class Four.
  'Of course it's not an island. It's the Isle of Portland, you dolts.'
  'Isle a Portant – ' Class Four looks confused.
  'Isle,' the twins say in a prim tone.

Bess has to admit it is an island, for the present at least. The causeway to the mainland is obscured by the fog – cut off by a fog as strong as the sea: thick, white, impossible to walk through. She looks round, near to despair.

Laurie, who was the first to step from the prow of the boat, is out of sight.

The disused quarry at the top of the cliff gives a strange view, a prehistoric vision, almost, of jagged boulders, uneven, bushy grass that could feed no domesticated animal like a cow or horse, and the sea no longer blue but wild and grey and running. Bess shudders, slithering on mud that's white, limestone mud.

'We 'ad a lady at Club with this.'

'Club. Yah. Pottery Club.'

Class Four are invigorated by the cold air, the breeze from the sea. They stamp about in the quarry, hugging anoraks tight to the body.

'I want that bit.'

'It's mine.'

The twins have helped Bess with the bedding and provisions, pulled wearily up the long steps. Bess thinks they'd have done better to stay on the beach. She calls to Jane, who is climbing in the quarry with the others – like a baby, Bess thinks in her tiredness. Jane comes down reluctantly.

'What?' It's going to be a service of some kind, demanded by an elder sister and not easily refused.

'We'd do better on the beach.' Bess's voice comes in short pants, like it does before she has a nervous coughing attack. 'It's too cold and windy up here.'

'It's not!' Jane is eager in her denial. 'It's lovely in there.' She points at the quarry. 'It's lovely. Honestly, it is.'

Layers of stone, shelves really, where coats and bedding can be spread out. The quarry must be about forty feet in height. Yes, it is sheltered: for a moment, Bess's spirits rise. They won't freeze to death tonight, at least. And in the centre is a round, charred circle where the quarry workers must have had a fire. Few sticks, in such a barren spot. But there is a whole tree, a small conifer, which has blown down on the west side of the quarry. Bess points at it.

'Drag that tree into the middle,' she calls out. 'We're going to have a fire.'

Class Four rush down from the ledges. Their sneakers are covered in white mud, and so are their hands and hair. They look like horror-comic ghosts, as they run for the tree, drag it into the centre and begin snapping off the branches.

'Guy Fawkes!'

'I'm going to light it!'

'*I'm* going to light it!'

'No, me!'

Sensible, practical Bess. With the packet of fire-lighters taken from the kiosk, and the bundle of newspapers she stuffed into the bags with the stale cheese and tomato sandwiches, she goes to the centre of the quarry. She thinks: It's strange how there should be a wind only a few feet away – a wind that won't go the three miles or so to the causeway, dispel the fog and connect us with the mainland – and won't come in here either, to this protected place. But for the time, she's grateful to do without.

'Melanie.'

Melanie is skulking on a ledge, about fifteen feet up. She doesn't like the tone of command she hears in Bess's voice, so she doesn't answer.

'Get Melanie.' Bess nudges Jane, who is enjoying the growing pyre of dead pine. 'She's got a lighter.'

Melanie, when it comes to it, enjoys being the

provider of fire. She likes fire anyway – the time, at Whitehays, when everyone was out except her and the cat, and the cat's tail got so burnt, with a lump of coal jumping out of the hearth right on to it. She kneels by the heap, rolled-gold lighter in hand. Class Four run up.

'Let me 'ave a go, Melanie!'

'Please.'

But Melanie has no intention of lending the lighter. She sees herself as indispensable, a thief no longer; she is the supplier of fire without which they would all perish.

Flames start small, nibble at the pine cones and give a burst of sparks at the first dry branches.

'Fireworks!'

'Bangers!'

The fire gets bigger, still low down, orange. Bess looks round and frowns when she sees that the group is yet again not complete. She turns to the twins, who as always are standing side by side and a few feet behind her.

'Where's – ' Her voice is cut off by a shout from Class Four.

'Witch!'

'I seen it when we was up in the London Dungeon. They burn them.'

'In the olden days.'

'No. Now.'

'Yeh. I seen it. They was burnin' them in the London Dungeon.'

The fire is high now, about ten feet high. At the top of the cliff – thirty feet above the fire, but by an odd, optical trick she looks as if she were tied to a stake at the top of the fire – there stands a dark-coated figure. Her hair is dark too, and sticks up at the side of her face because she is directly in the wind.'

'Laurie.' The twins answer Bess together. And, of course, Bess has seen her by now. That black figure, black as a witch, over the flames going higher from the fire.

'It's Laurie.'

No one listens, in the excitement of the burning witch.

Nine

The Journal of Laurence Lelandes

> What am I, a life without meaning?
> A nought, a heart in play,
> Unwished-for ghost,
> Conductor of hard feeling,
> Nested here but cannot fly away . . .
> *Mary, Queen of Scots*

M Y MOTHER IS calling out to me . . . but I can't get closer. She's in the kitchen, the part of the house with walls the colour of a cooking apple, the crude part of the house where the Monsieur sends his orders but never comes. He might want carp, or a peach on its own on a mother of pearl plate! A bell carries his demands, in a thin wire that has been painted over crudely too, tacked to the wall the colour of unripe green. My mother wipes her hands on her apron. Her hands are either too dry, dusted over with flour, or they are damp, from always going in the wooden sink, and out again. When she has wiped her hands, she pats her hair. She leaves our part of the house and goes to the door that leads through to Monsieur. What can I hear? Racquets – the trot of balls – my mother's voice, asking Monsieur what he would like.

The sea out here is waiting to take me to France. The waves are little paper boats – and when the wind gets up, the boats will grow and the white cones will fill out to sails. A ship will be waiting for me down in the cove, with sails like the head-dresses they wear on feast-days, in Rouen. I step in, and we're blown across the sea . . . we nudge the coast at Cherbourg and we go up-river, an ivory boat that makes the farmers stare. Fat brown and white cows, you look as if you had been painted on the three-cornered fields by an artist who would rather be in the South Seas.

But I will drown. Long before we dock in the shallow river at the bottom of the field that is Monsieur's park, with its wide trees and nibbled grass and a cut of brown water running under unsteady planks, I will have fallen from the sides of the ship and gone in a cloud of sea-air, down. The black I wear will turn to white, the white mourning of the French Court. But my mother will go on putting her hands in the wooden sink, and pulling them out again. And she'll wipe them on her white apron, while I go down and down in the water – in the suds of the sea – and the ship will unfurl and go down, until it's only a piece of white paper again, frayed, ready to frill the smart new cutlets my mother will serve to Monsieur.

Now I am here I shall drown. At the back of us is a white mist that will cover and explore us, poke up our noses and into our lungs. The only place to run is the sea. But I feel a hand pushing . . . a hand on my shoulder blades . . . I turn and see *her* face, cheeks tinged with triumph, red hair nearly gold, like the haloes of saints in the stained-glass windows at home. Then she draws back . . . Or am I dreaming, in this place away from the rest, this hole in the side of the hill, a cave with a white boulder at the mouth, like the entrance to a tomb? Did I really see her, gold hair flying past, first warning that she will be the one to throw me down into the sea?

Ten

'WHERE'S LAURIE?'
Jane sits on the highest, widest ledge with Bess. The fire still burns brightly below them. Sunday afternoon, sea and sky enamel calm, a brochure sun with no hint of a sudden six o'clock extinction. Only, Bess is frowning: Jane can see she worries for them all.

'L-Laurie?' Jane tenses with the effort of speech, as if it were a horse bucking under her, having to be reined in.

'I dunno. S-somewhere.'

Above, an odd, local wind teases at the scratchy bushes and makes the yellowing grass stand up on end. Jane lies back against the duvet they took from the hut. Her eyes close. In some ways it's nicer here than at home – there's no need to prove how keen you are: keen on sports and gymkhanas and all the things that keep you out of the home, away from the cushiony smell Mrs Plantain has made for herself and now regrets.

In a deep cavity low in the quarry, Class Four are bundled, munching. Someone found marshmallows in the kiosk: they've been toasted and eaten. The fire gives a comforting heat. Only one is letting out sobs. She is small, with yellow bunches straggling free of elastic bands. Two others prop her between them, on a blanket smelling of rotten fish. 'It's the Wind Man.' Melanie is in charge of the group. 'Look! 'E's up there! 'E'll make yer better. Blow it away!'

No one much believes her. There is no Wind Man to be seen, only the bushes blowing about like scarecrows at the top of the cliff. Not a cloud in sight, to be kicked across the sky by the Wind Man.

'What's 'e do, then?' says one of Class Four, out of politeness.

' 'E's mostly bad.' Melanie eyes the victim, decides she can bear it, or anyway that she has to. ' 'E throws people off ladders. Takes babies outa cots –'

'Takes babies – ' Class Four show a glimmer of interest.

'Oh yah. Someone I know – ' Melanie pauses for effect.

'What then?'

'Put 'er baby out on the lawn – '

'What lawn?'

Melanie stops, annoyed, then resumes. 'O.K., I'll tell yer. White'ays Estate.'

'Go on.'

'Yer tellin' a lie, Mel'nie.'

'Then what happened?' The quiet, almost-sobbing voice of the girl with bunches.

67

'Who cares?' Melanie makes a show of huffiness.

'Go on.'

'Please.'

'Wot'd 'e do with the baby?'

'Changed it.'

'What?'

Melanie shows impatience. She glances up the cliff. There are Bess and Jane sprawled on the high ledge, as if they are out on a picnic. The twins are sitting lower down, where they have found a colony of snails. Each twin holds a snail – from where Melanie stands, she sees their little eyes in their white faces, and held up under their chins, like pets, the snails. Nat is crouched by the fire, feeding it with twigs and leaves and staring into the flames.

'Changed it with what?' Class Four, on their knees in the limy dust, shuffle up to Melanie.

'Bet it's a monster.'

'I don't want to see the Wind Man.'

'Fer another baby, 'f course.' Melanie looks down at her audience in contempt.

'What's 'e done that for?'

' 'E just changes them over. Puts in someone else's baby.'

A hush falls. Not one in the group fails to see herself suddenly transported, taken in giant strides across the sky in the arms of the Wind Man. Out of his great, windy sleeves they fall into the world of chance, the happy childhood gone at a blow to misery, poverty, neglect.

' 'Oo did 'e do it with?' A subdued voice, at last.

' 'Er.' Melanie jerks her thumb. They all stare up at the ledge. At the same time, as if in obedience to Melanie's powers, the wind gains strength. It jumps down from the bushes and dances round the fire. The fire heaves sideways, taken unawares. Its round red mouth of flame nearly scorches Nat, who cries out.

'Bess?' The girls look in disbelief at the ledge. Who could imagine Bess ever to have been changed with anyone: Bess, who knows where she belongs? Even Bess's red-gold hair marks her as special, she could never be a baby snatched up from a pram and thrown into a magpie's nest.

'No. Course not. 'Er.'

Well, Jane does make more sense. In fact, as soon as the thought presents itself, Class Four see Jane lying in the pram on a lawn at an unknown house and the scooping arm of the Wind Man pulling her sideways from under the hood. There – through the air she goes – they see her dumped down at Forton Court, in a flowerbed filled with tulips.

' 'Oo'd he change 'er with then?'

Melanie turns and faces the wind. It puffs out her frizzy hair, and the glare from the later afternoon sun makes her close her eyes, which are so deep-set they look as if they have vanished altogether, sewn under white skin. The fire has made a bright blush on her pasty cheeks. She stretches out her arms, dramatically.

'Me.'

Eleven

Nat, who has heard some of this, pulls herself away from the fire. She has become hypnotised by the fire, Melanie's words have gone easily and smoothly in, she has seen in the flames Melanie's flight in the arms of the Wind Man, her banishment from the cool halls of Forton Court. Looking up she sees Jane, pony-owner, swinging her legs on the best ledge with a girl who isn't her real sister.

'I'm goin' to tell 'er,' says a voice from the group.

Melanie swings round. But before she can intervene, a natural disaster is discovered and the matter put to the side.

The girl with the bunches, the crying one who was only temporarily quieted by the tale of changelings, has been seen to have a cluster of large, blister spots. Two of the girls kneel beside her: she is lying on a duffle coat now, under the low ceiling of the ledge.

The spots are on the chest, and there are two or three which have come up bang in the middle of the left cheek. Melanie, who has undisputed leadership now, strides over, doctorly.

'Let me see, please.'

The victim, sobbing again, shows the portion of

chest where these eruptions, like medieval towers on the white plain of the skin, have suddenly thrust up. Melanie whistles, then changes it for an experienced cough.

'Yes. There's a lot of it about.'

The girls are calmer for a moment. Most ailments in the village, or at school, are 'a-lot-of-it-about'.

Melanie stalks the patient. She turns, all eyes on her, and beckons to Nat.

'Can you come here a moment, please, Nurse?'

Nat walks forward. She feels the familiar tingle of pretend-games, the heady sensation that things can any moment topple over and go out of control.

'Yes, Doctor?'

The faces of Class Four are turned to this hospital scene. Bess and Jane, and the twins on their separate ledges, are like spectators in the amphitheatre.

'Get the . . . um . . . syringe, please Nurse.'

Nat bends down, scrabbles for a twig, holds it out.

'We got to get rid a these things before it's too late, see? It's the plague.'

Twelve

NIGHT FALLS. OR rather, it creeps up beside the sun, which is red again and spilling red light on the stones, the girls on their ledges and in the low-ceilinged cavern under the last ledge of the quarry – it makes the fire dull, the sun's last burst of red before going out. A sharp wind from the sea still blows. Night covers the wall of fog; but there are no lights twinkling on the coast, as there would be if the fog had gone. And the only stars are over the island of boulders that look like broken-off columns in the short grass pitted with quarries. Where the fog is, there are no stars. Only here, over the sea and the beaches of giant pebbles, stars are bright in the clear black: from time to time they seem to swoop and fall, as if to make up for the white seabirds that have been silent and invisible all day.

Bess's red hair has gone dull, too, with the darkness. When she sat on the highest ledge, feet sticking out and skirt pulled down, she could have been a girl in a painting by Millais: there's her hair, and a face people have called pre-Raphaelite, over a body beginning to curve. Even a pout – but it may have been an expression of fear. Now, she has swung down to the quarry floor and she looks ordinary, tired. What will there be to eat tomorrow, if tonight sees the last of the sweets and the stale bread? The second night out has taken her too far away, into this island of stones and girls chattering as if minutes and miles had never been made. Do they think they'll wake safely in bed, and all this was a tale told them before sleep? Or don't they think at all? Bess knows that only the twins, who stand uncertainly by the fire, and her sister Jane, have any idea of the reality. And she feels fear, stooping to look in at the low cavern and finding herself answered by the shining eyes of Class Four – eyes without memory, or care.

Jane comes out of the cavern. Bess can tell immediately that she has slid back in age as she does sometimes at home when she doesn't get her way. Rage has whitened her face: freckles stand out on her nose as if they had just been painted there.

'They won't let me!'

Bess stoops lower, she is too tall to go in the cavern without crawling.

'Let you what?'

'I want to run the hospital. It's my turn. They won't let me!'

One of Class Four runs to Bess, grabs her knees.

'I was homesick! I cried!'

'I cried too!'

'I'm sorry I cried.'

So they had remembered, for a short time. That they aren't at home – that the hospital, where Bess now sees one child lying very still, in a bundle of old blankets from the kiosk – isn't a hospital at all, but a cold limestone floor with the wind blowing in and only the light from the fire to see by. Or can they remember only that they cried? Bess goes down on her knees and makes for the ill child. Fear, already waiting, now pounces close: Bess sweats as she goes on grazed knees to the far end of the cavern.

'No one wants you to run this hospital.' Melanie's voice is loud and positive. 'You just take orders, Nurse.'

'It's not fair!' Despite her age, despite the boyish qualities of empire-building Aunt Gertie, Jane bursts into tears. 'I'm Matron,' she says. Melanie laughs.

The child with the spots has been given a can of Fanta, several injections with a twig dipped in Coke, a facial operation, comprising charcoal lines drawn across the cheeks. A box of wax crayons has been used to draw blue and red circles round the affected parts.

'It's the plague.' Melanie strides up behind Bess. 'I'm runnin' the 'ospital. Get that bloody twirp outa 'ere.'

Jane's sobs come to the patient's bed, under a shelf of dank stone.

'Tell her to go away, Bess. Please!'

The ill child opens her eyes, which are glued with a yellow phlegm. The watery eyes show pupils tiny, wandering, like tadpoles going round.

'Will you be quiet!' Bess puts her mother's

authority into her voice. But she has to crawl backwards to get out and Melanie laughs again.

'It's nothing serious.'

Even as she speaks, Bess knows she doesn't know. The spots look like the flea bites a girl had at school – she remembers the jokes, and the fumigation of the dormitory. On the other hand, would anyone with flea bites be as ill as that? There was the effect of the walk, of course, and the shock of being away from home . . . Bess must be showing her uncertainty, for as she reaches the open air, Melanie follows and pulls roughly at her arm.

'It's the plague. I'm lookin' after 'er!' She pulls a messy bundle from her pocket and holds it up. 'I got the medicine.' She points angrily at Jane, who has also come out into the open, by the fire that needs more wood or it will shortly go out.

'What?' Bess stares, distracted. Jane's face, still white, looms up at her. 'Can't you give her a turn?' Bess says, and already she knows she sounds like the weakest teacher at school. Melanie is winning; Jane is a furious infant; most of Class Four have stumbled out now, to take Melanie's side. 'What is that?' . . . she plays for time, as the bundle of faded grasses is waved in her face.

' 'Erbs.' Melanie's tone is triumphant. 'For the plague.'

Class Four crows approval. 'Yeah.' Then, as Bess stands undecided, a voice comes up:

'Mel'nie was changed. They come an' take 'er

75

away, din' they?'
  Another voice, more doubtful:
  'Was it real?'
  'Yeah. She was changed.'
Except for the doubtful one, a loud corroboration:
  'The Wind Man. 'E took 'er outa the pram at your
'ome an' . . . '
  'Swopped 'er – '
  'With Jane. It's not fair.'

Bess searches for the twins. This is impossible, this
tale of changelings in an abandoned quarry where
one child is already seriously ill and where they may
all soon starve or die of exposure. She curses Melanie – and she curses the Walks Woman, whose idea
of a 'mixed walk' from different schools this had
been. Melanie and Jane hate each other anyway –
but to include Class Four of the village school, and
the comp. – when she could have had control of the
situation by now, with friends from Ferndale and,
best of all, Miss Knowles. The twins are hardly old
enough to provide sanity . . . yet surely . . . '

Mary and Mathilda stand silent by the edge of the
fire. It's the first they've heard of the changeling
theory, as they were collecting snails high up in the
quarry when Melanie broke the news. And their
silence is one of incomprehension: they see each
other, alone in prams, exchanged for the other and
always the same. Somewhere in their minds they
join, and are together again, in the double life they
have always known. To be different, to be taken

away from the other, is unthinkable.

'Mary. Mathilda.' Bess walks over to them. 'This is all nonsense. Isn't it?'

The twins are practical. They see Bess is at the end of her tether, and that the fire is about to go out. Mary speaks first.

'It's not possible.' Then Mathilda:

'There's a dead tree up at the top of the quarry. If everyone comes, we can drag it down for the fire.'

'You hear that? It's impossible.' Bess turns to Class Four, to the faces like puppets' faces gazing up at her.

'But wot about the Wind Man?'

Bess begins to lose her temper. It occurs to her that she might walk off now, go anywhere, into the fog if necessary.

'There is no Wind Man,' she says.

Thirteen

IT'S UNFORTUNATE THAT just then two things happened, and that both happened at the same time. The first was an idea — that came to Mary and then to Mathilda, and was sent from their father, the memory of their father as he stood before them in the small, book-lined room in the house behind the school.

'You could have two people exactly the same – ' Mary began.

'Everyone is born the same,' said Mathilda.

'And – what they're like is depending on where they're brought up,' said Mary.

'In a capitalist society,' Mathilda finished off.

A silence. The eyes of Class Four swivel to the twins. Understanding nothing, they nevertheless surmise that the rich Plantains, whose accents are often mocked in the village, have paid the Wind Man to snatch Melanie from her desirable garden at Forton Court and put her down on the lawn at Whitehays. Jane, who really should have been at Whitehays all along, has been brandishing tennis racquets illegally come by, waving at village children from the back of a private horse. They might feel sorry for her – but they don't. She has even given the impression of enjoying her dishonest life.

'Really – ' Bess starts up. But it's too late. As Class Four go into their chant again, of It's not fair, and It's Melanie's 'Ospital, the second unfortunate thing occurs. It's the wind, blowing in sudden sharp gusts, scattering the ashes of the fire so that Class Four has to jump out of the way. A sock is singed, an ankle briefly stung, as if a swarm of fiery wasps has darted out of the fire.

'It's the Wind Man!'

' 'E's comin' to get us!'

By the time Bess has pushed the children back into the cavern, the twins have disappeared up the quarry to bring down the tree. When they return, with Bess and Jane standing over the embers and Class Four wailing inside at Melanie's spooky voice and more ghostly tales, Bess has already seen the only way out. It won't be escape, of course – steady, sensible Bess could never leave her charges just like that. Rock-like Bess, her mother says. You can't upset Bess. So, as she and Jane and the twins jump on the dead tree and break it up for the fire, she calls out for Melanie. Again, she curses the Walks Woman who has brought them all to this.

'You called, Madam?'

Flushed, Melanie appears by the fire. She holds her hands out as if serving, balancing a tray. She doesn't get a laugh – Class Four is too terrified for that.

'Melanie – where is that – that girl?'

Melanie doesn't answer at first. She helps with the fire, throwing in a branch of withered leaves. A crackling comes up out of the fire.

'Oh. You mean – Laurie?' Melanie shrugs, indifferent. 'Prob'ly went 'ome for all I know.'

But the twins aren't laughing either. Melanie can feel the tension, like at home when she goes too far. She decides, all at once, to give in.

'She's in – well – I know where she is.' All the same, it's a secret: Melanie smirks with self-importance.

'Get her then.'

'Oh. O.K.'

Melanie goes off, but very slowly and dragging the toes of her sneakers along the ground. Her back view shows amazement at the request, and satisfaction that Bess has admitted she has no one of her own age to confide in, no one here she can trust. Out of the circle of the fire, she vanishes from sight.

The moon – a fraction fuller than the half-moon of the night before – rises in the sky. Melanie has left the quarry and gone southwards, on a narrow path that leads down to the sea.

Fourteen

THE CAVE WAS just above sea-level, jutting out over a beach where the round, outsize stones, in the faint glow from the moon, lay piled together like the backs of sleeping tortoises. A small boulder, whitish, stood against the mouth of the cave. The path stopped suddenly about twenty feet short of the boulder and Melanie slid towards it over balding grass and limestone dust: only this, noisily grabbed and rocking slightly at the impact of her weight, prevented a last rush into the sea.

The noise seemed to have made no difference to

Laurie, who sat just inside the entrance to the cave. Her knees were drawn up under her chin, her head was bent down on her knees. Melanie, puffing and hearing the exaggerated beat of her heart and dull rhythm of the sea, peered in through the crack between the boulder and the side of the cliff. Laurie faced the boulder, and the cave was dark except for some moonlight which came in on the far side. Melanie could make out the hunched figure in the black coat, and by her feet on the ground the white missal. As Laurie still made no movement, Melanie stayed quiet. She suspected Laurie was praying to the powerful white book – and she knew when she was in the presence of a force, because an odd, misty light would come, and this light was there now, streaming in round the boulder. When the light came, things usually flew about or rose with a terrible inevitability and hurled themselves in what-ever direction was least probable. Clinging to the boulder, Melanie felt it for an instant tremble on the ledge. She felt no fear, she never did when the paralysing white light was there, but she prayed too: to the white thing that was the most powerful destructive weapon ever invented, the weapon which Laurie had only to throw out into the sea for the world to go up in a puffball of deadly smoke.

Laurie picked up the book. The white, vaporous air grew thicker in the cave. Melanie's breath came in short, even bursts, so loud it took the place of the sea – as if all the waves, and the salt water running in obedience to the tides, sang to the order of her pumping lungs. Laurie opened the book. There was the sound of thin, very crinkly paper being riffled through. Melanie frowned. In the half-light she saw Laurie's long fingers place a bookmark – or it could have been a pen, it was hard to see – in the pages. The bomb must be buried deep in the paper thin as the communion wafers Melanie had seen Ms·Potts eat when she had made her go with her to church. It must be lying there, in a nest of white, shredded paper, and Laurie would take it out, talk to it and tell it what to do, as Melanie sometimes did with one object or another when there had been no misty light for a time and she wanted things to cause trouble again.

Laurie closed the book. She looked up, and straight into Melanie's eyes, fixed like a cat's in the chink at the side of the boulder. The whitish light faded away. Melanie felt no force at all, at the dark entrance to the dark cave where the moon, wrapped in trailing clouds, no longer shone.

'Laurie,' Melanie's voice went straight into stone. She could only see Laurie's pale face now, made thin and long by the black hair that was invisible in the blackness of the cave.

'Laurie – can I come in?'

As soon as Melanie spoke, she knew she couldn't. Laurie was quite still, but this time the breathing of the sea seemed to come from her, as if she were sighing in exasperation. Melanie felt guilt – and then rage, at Bess for making her come and incur Laurie's anger. She moved the side of her face against the cliff so that her mouth could go in the chink, with one eye above looking in. The clouds slipped off the moon and a faint light came again – but it wasn't the light of Melanie's force, when something was bound to happen.

'I'm sorry. I'm sorry.'

Laurie could have been watching Melanie's mouth, as it wiggled by the side of the cliff. Or she could simply be listening to the sound of the sea. The pale face, like a white medallion, hung over the missal in the ivory binding, on knees shrouded and almost invisible in the black coat.

'I won't tell,' Melanie said. A tear oozed out of the eye and ran down to the lips. 'I promise.'

Laurie's hand came out of the folds of the coat, the other still gripped the missal. A long, white finger came up to the boulder, brushed the rough stone and landed gently on Melanie's lips. The tear was absorbed by the finger, then the finger pressed down a moment, as if to admonish, or to ensure silence. Melanie pulled away. With her face freed, she thrust a hand into the dark aperture. She stared up at the moon, which lolloped over the waves, still held on a white filament of cloud. The finger inside coiled round hers. Then it let go, and there was still silence. Melanie crawled up the cliff, holding on to rock, to the roots of half-dead bushes that gave off a hiss of crumbling stones as she went. By the time she found the path and looked down at the cave and the boulder, they were small, only part of the rock over the sea. The moon came down on the whitish boulder which lay like a stone falling from its setting, in the bracelet of rocks and stones by the sea.

Bess had shared out the last of the Opal Fruits, and the stuck-together toffees, and the crumbling egg sandwiches from the kiosk, refused earlier and now munched ravenously, with what was left of the Coke and Fanta to wash it down. She had told Class Four that hospitals could no longer be played and that the ill child should sleep near the fire: a wigwam of bedding erected on twigs had been placed over her. She had told Nat to stop fussing, when she complained of having to sleep on a ledge near the twins – Nat had said they would give her bad dreams. She had comforted Jane, who was embarrassed at her babyish behaviour with Melanie, and had tried to tell her that the fog would lift tomorrow, the wind must blow it away, and they would all be home by lunch. But Jane hadn't believed her. A despondency had come down on the quarry, under a racing moon that by its wild, frivolous movement made the place all the lonelier. The wind lifted duffle coats, spat into the fire and darted off again. Out at sea, dancing to the wind, small white waves charged and receded.

Bess stands at the edge of the quarry, looking down at the sea. In the relative calm of the quarry above the cove and the beach, she sees her class at school, moving in the faint light over the water, against a blackboard of night. She hears the voice of Miss

Knowles, in the sharp rapping wind as it rises and falls.

Fifteen

Miss Knowles had told them of the court of the first Elizabeth – of formal gardens planted with a lexicon of herbs, of tapestries where the red thread that made a gash of stag's blood was still bright in the woven forests on the walls. The Armada, sails like an angry porcupine, coming in to easy defeat – men with ruffs, sailors, poets – banquets with girls singing in green-sleeved dresses, and swans, glazed and jewelled, that gave forth tiny birds, down to the ortolan. The Virgin Queen in a dress like the Eiffel Tower. A cold, white bosom and a neck as long as a swan's, in a white ruff of angry feathers as she guarded, day and night, her virginity. Pearls no bigger than grains of sand dotted her red hair – like snow, white seed pearls in a strict bodice kept her heart cold. She goes always slowly, walking as if the ground under her can never be firm, as if water lies just under the ground and makes it swell. In the grey sea, in and out of the grey rose-bushes of her distant garden, Queen Bess walks, her skirts flaring in spray. The moon sails above a shadowy topiary of clouds. The wise Queen turns her face to land and the moon's rays frizzle out behind her – like hair, like the gold-stitched train of her robe. Courtiers bow, and dance to music lost under the sea. Ruffs show white, with the night sky coming in. Bess can see eyes, and a round face or a long face, olive-skinned, or with a pointed beard. In the dancing girls she sees her friends – laughing with the pleasure of being padded out in velvet and lace – sweep down to her, good Queen Bess. It seems the moods of the sea depend on her. *Semper eadem*, the motto of the Virgin Queen. Always the same.

Bess turns suddenly – the moon is stabbed behind a panel of black sky and goes out. The sea has nothing but the soft, grey roll, ladies tumbling in their silks, bottoms up and lace flying in the concealing night. She is alone on the cliff – but she can dimly see Melanie, making her way panting up the stony path.

'Well, where is she?' Bess sees nothing behind Melanie but night.

'She won't come.'

Melanie arrives beside Bess. Her snorting breath has a victorious note. She looks up at Bess's impassive face and, wisely, hides a smile.

'She won't come?' Bess speaks almost to herself, almost in disbelief.

'Where is she then?' It is worse than a dream, this palace of stone with two sides to it: one black, the night sky of the West, and the other white, fog, obscuring the hope of morning. Bess turns, she will

86

go and find Jane, between them they will work it out, without Laurie. But before she goes, she says once more to Melanie:

'Where is she?'

Melanie gives Bess a sly look and then looks down again, at the hazily visible ground.

'It's a secret,' she says.

Report by Ms S. B. Potts on Melanie Ayres (continued):

Shortly before the walk of October 17th, reports came from neighbours at Whitehays of excessive disturbances in the Ayres household. Both Miss Clews, and Mr Bartram, who are in the immediate vicinity of the Ayreses, complained often of loud music 'at about 2 a.m.' and twice of large pieces of furniture being hurled from the first floor window to the accompaniment of music (sometimes classical, sometimes pop) being played at an intolerable pitch. Miss Clews adds that a complete silence is liable to follow, that lights go out on the first floor, and that shortly afterwards the figure of Mr Ayres can be seen leaving the house. He goes to the end of the road in the council estate and is then seen to enter the bus shelter. Miss Clews has on both occasions heard the sound of female laughter emanating from the shelter, followed by sounds she has said she would prefer not to describe. Mr Bartram, who has recently been fitted with a hearing aid, remarks only that as soon as the figure of the man (whom he supposes to be Mr Ayres) leaves the house and reaches the end of the road, he is incapable of hearing further. Mr Bartram has seen the entry into the bus shelter of Mr Ayres on the same occasions as those reported by Miss Clews.

Mrs Ayres refused either myself or my colleagues access to the house. I visited Melanie at school, therefore, and we talked in the break. Melanie at first refused to confirm additional disturbances, but on my suggesting that the best way for me to find out if she was telling the truth or not would be to go that evening to the bus shelter, she broke down and admitted that 'they' were back in force and that 'they' had driven her to run into her parents' first floor bedroom when everyone was asleep – as she did so, lights came on and loud music played; inevitably furniture was thrown about and the scene ended in her father leaving the house. I asked her where he went.

'None of your business,' was Melanie's reply. Then, 'Not as far as I'm going this Saturday, I'll tell you.'

It is of course to be regretted that this threat of running away was not sufficiently registered at the time – however, events have proved the oversight to have different consequences from those at first foreseen; had the organiser of the walk been asked to keep a special eye on Melanie, it is perhaps possible that she would not have strayed so far from the girls and would have steered them away from danger. It might also be supposed that Melanie is safer now, with a group, than she would have been on her own. This is optimistic thinking, of course, and we await developments as anxiously here as do the parents of the group members.

To return to the recent outbreak of violence at Whitehays, it seems probable that Mr Ayres was keeping a rendezvous with a woman in the bus shelter and that Melanie resisted this with all the 'forces' she appears to have at her disposal. I asked her if she had followed her father on any of these occasions, to which she replied, 'Once to Bridport.' Neither my colleague nor I can make out the meaning of this, as buses in this part of the country do not of course run at that hour of the morning. It also seems unlikely that Mr Ayres and his companion would choose to walk five miles to Bridport at that hour and for no apparent reason. Melanie refused to elucidate her meaning, however. Since her departure on the walk, calm has prevailed at Whitehays. Miss Clews, whose dog has needed to be taken out in the early hours of the morning throughout the past week, has reported an absence of occupation of the bus shelter and a corresponding absence of noise, although she tells us that the dog becomes particularly excited at the entrance to the bus shelter and that it is difficult to drag him away from the spot.

Mr Bartram, who says he is woken regularly by Miss Clews's night walks with the dog, claims on the other hand that he has twice seen a figure whom he supposes to be Mr Ayres leave the front door and make his way down the road. Whichever is the case, loud music and furniture-throwing are no longer taking place at the Ayres household in Whitehays.

Sixteen

'I'M COLD.'
'You're pulling it all your side.'
'It's not fair.'
'When is it morning time?'

Nat lies in the quarry between Class Four and the twins. At first, she thought the wriggling, crying and complaining of the little ones in the cave worse than the quiet, sibilant talk of the twins, as they pore over their miniature chessboard. Now, she is as used to the murmurings of Class Four as a mother sow is to her tiresome litter – comforted by it, even. What is unbearable is the low, calculating conversation of Mary and Mathilda, in their working out of their moves, the safety of their future.

'Water,' Mary is saying. 'You saw the big drum-thing, didn't you?'

'Yes. Of course.'

'Up over there – '

'I put my finger in it.'

'I know.'

'It's clean. And pure.'

'But what do we put it in?'

'What do you think?'

'Oh yes. The thermos Melanie took from the kiosk.'

'Melanie. We need the thermos.'

'Yes. We could pay her.'

'With Opal Fruits.'

'Yes. How many did you take?'

'Same as you.'

'From the girl – '

'She won't need them.'

'No one eats sweet when they're sick.'

Nat feels pinpricks of shame, at listening. What are the twins not capable of, when they rob an ill child and prepare to creep off to a secret supply of water? Should she tell Bess? Bess, she sees, is standing at the edge of the quarry, looking out to sea. What does she watch, on the dull waves ruled with a lead pencil on grey paper? The moon has gone behind the sky and doesn't show even the tip of a pointed chin – earlier Nat had thought of her mother, and the book with the cow jumping over a moon with the face of an old woman. But now there are only a few stars and a faint light the colour of fishbones from the sea.

Nat decides not to disturb Bess. She looks as if she is thinking too hard. But the twins are planning and plotting – and soon Nat realises what it is they plan to do.

'It's more comfortable up there.'

'Nearer the water.'

'We could pick up Melanie's thermos on the way.'

'Without even waking her.'

'Bess'll be happier down here.'

'What about Jane?'

'She can come down here too.'

'But she's alseep.'

'We can carry her between us.'

'Ah.'

'You mean – '

'Yes. Put Melanie up there.'

'Where Jane was.'

'But when Melanie wakes up and her thermos is gone – '

'She'll be in a different place anyway. She was sleepwalking.'

'And she dropped it.'

'Yes. And Jane – '

'Will think she's – '

'Yes. Been changed – '

'With Melanie.'

'By the Wind Man.'

Laughter. Cold laughter, like ice shaking together. Silence, as a pawn is taken or a knight moved on the tiny board. Nat shifts on the stones. But now she feels guilt, in listening. The twins must have picked this up, for now two small, round heads peer suddenly close to her in the darkness. Nat feigns sleep.

'It's O.K. She's asleep.'

'I don't think she is.'

'No. But she won't get in our way.'

It's true, a few minutes later Nat has wandered to the half-sleeping state that comes so often to her these days. She doesn't see Bess, as Bess leaves the edge of the quarry and climbs up the side to her place at the top. She sees her father, in a sudden shaft of brilliant moonlight that comes down on Chesil Bank like a diamond pin in a hat. Nat's father is standing, exhausted and white but there – there to repel the visits from the twins and their father, there to make life interesting at home again. Nat struggles to a half-sitting position. Her eyes half-open, showing two triangles of pupil-less expanse, glaucous-looking and grey.

As the twins wait for Bess to go to sleep before they carry out their plan of abductions, their rise to the top, Nat pulls herself to her feet and her feet begin to move. The twins are too busy whispering to hear her. And they are too engrossed, as they lie face to face in their pod of duffle and scarves, in the self and the other, to see Nat go across the dull white of the quarry floor and down the steep path to the boat they'd all heaved up yesterday, as far up the stones as it would go.

Clinical Report on Bess Plantain (continued):

It soon became clear — and would have considerably facilitated an understanding of the case, had not treatment abruptly terminated in the week before the walk of Saturday October 17th — that life at Forton Court was a good deal more complicated than it at first appeared.

For, on the second occasion of our meeting, it transpired that Bess's feeling for her mother had been almost completely repressed and that great emphasis had been placed on the role of Mrs Strang, the housekeeper of a year's standing.

Mrs Strang, in the space of a few months, had taken over from Mrs Plantain with great efficiency. As Mrs Plantain found almost any physical effort beyond her capacity, Mrs Strang was called on to cook and serve, supervise the cleaning of the house, arrange flowers, etc. She was allotted quarters at the back of the house, overlooking the courtyard: this was the old 'servants' wing'; and she was always punctilious in returning there when her duties were done, though Bess remarked that it was strange how often the cushions in the main hall needed to be resewn *in situ*. What Bess meant by this, of course, was that Mrs Strang was quite often not to be found in her own quarters; soon it began to emerge that she had been found in a bedroom in the main part of the house – and then, within a matter of weeks, in another.

Mr Plantain was in the habit of going twice a year to Scotland, where a friend ran a 'hydro': here he relaxed, took courses of massage and hydrotherapy for his injury – and, as Bess had no difficulty in assuring me, enjoyed his temporary separation from his wife. In the August of this year – that is, two months before the walk of Saturday October 17th, Mr Plantain went as usual to the Scottish moors; and Mrs Plantain's stepbrother, 'Uncle' to Bess, was seen by the child in bed with Mrs Strang. Bess was quick to tell her father of this on his return: there appear to have been a succession of rows, as a result of which Mrs Plantain's stepbrother left the house, and on the surface things went on much as before. It appears, however, that the hurt inflicted on Bess at this time was greater than a mere blow to the pride, occasioned by a former (discarded) suitor, 'Uncle', going off in pursuit of Mrs Strang. It became a matter of urgency to discover the 'secret' which Bess, in common with so many neurotics, was determined to defend to the last.

The first place to look, as I have found so often in cases of hysterical girls manifesting such symptoms, is in the relationship between the girl and her father. We have ascertained already that the impotence, supposed or actual, of Mr Plantain had occupied much of Bess's imaginative life. The obvious lack of any marital relationship with the mother had drawn father and daughter close together. On the occasion of 'Uncle's' approach in the hayloft, Bess had been happy to think of 'Uncle' receiving punishment from Mr Plantain's riding crop. She had told her father of the incident – as, indeed, she had hastened to tell him of 'Uncle' and Mrs Strang found together in an upper bedroom. On hearing of 'Uncle's' attempt to seduce his daughter, Mr Plantain had indeed threatened the riding crop – and even the police, until Mrs Plantain, who was extremely attached to her stepbrother, begged him to refrain from going so far. On the occasion of 'Uncle' and Mrs Strang being discovered, however, Mr Plantain had shown a different reaction. 'Uncle' had certainly been sent packing, as had been threatened at the time of his attempted seduction of Bess, but Mr Plantain had continued to show coldness and annoyance long after his departure – and this hostility, which continued through the end of August and the beginning of the September term at Ferndale, was directed at Bess.

As Bess explained with great difficulty – and twisting a jade necklace she frequently wore (I have on countless occasions perceived that a necklace, locket or crucifix twisted between the fingers is an almost infallible sign that the truth is in the process of being repressed) – there had never been coldness between herself and her father before. I pointed out to her, however, and she was bound to agree, that she had noticed, and felt keenly, a withdrawal of a close

96

physical affection on her father's part, at the time of her twelfth birthday. He had, despite this, always shown a scrupulousness in his dealings with her, and in particular over those disagreements between Bess and her mother which, as Bess grew older, flared up more and more often. If Bess had felt 'orphaned', as she once put it in her first analysis on being asked to describe the effect of her father's turning away from her, she now felt misused, misjudged and positively maltreated. Mr Plantain had ordered her to her room on several occasions, a punishment never before inflicted. He also 'went for long drives in the car' without her – and this Bess seemed to find most painful of all.

The situation, which seemed at this point to have grown distinctly obscure, was clarified to a certain extent when I asked Bess where these drives, which she missed so keenly, were likely to have taken him. 'As far as the Swannery at Abbotsbury perhaps,' was the reply. 'Or to the Gardens . . . ' – she meant the Sub-Tropical Gardens in those parts, I was able to ascertain. It transpired that in her earlier childhood, before Mr Plantain's withdrawal of affection, drives down the coast had given great happiness to both; Mrs Plantain had not felt inclined to join them, as she preferred to go shopping in Dorchester, or to go up to London, for her pleasure; and father and daughter had known a bond of shared exploration and discovery in these expeditions.

I repeated, therefore, Bess's words to her – that she supposed her father to have gone off purposely on these desirable drives on his own, after her revelation of the happenings at Forton Court in his absence: that he had deliberately excluded her, to show his disapproval, perhaps, of her aptitude for telling tales, however reprehensible Mrs Plantain's stepbrother's actions may have been.

It was on the second time of saying the word 'Abbotsbury' that my patient broke down, sobbing uncontrollably and twisting at the jade necklet until I thought she would snap it from its chain. When she was finally helped to calm down, she would only say there were swans at Abbotsbury, and that this was what had upset her. On my pressing her for the reasons for this, and also on asking again and much more sternly, if she were positive that this was the first occasion of a definite hostility to her on the part of her father (for this was when the jade had first started to twirl), Bess remained determinedly the same in her answers. Simply that 'something about swans' was upsetting to her – and that Mr Plantain had definitely not 'treated her unfairly' at any time in the past.

It is possible that in the early days of psycho-analysis an interpretation of an hysterical girl's disgust and fear of swans would have been sought in the myth of Leda and the Swan. Copulation with this strong, fierce bird, leading to impregnation and the producing of an egg, would have been seen to reflect a secret fear of masturbation: of the egg's maturing in the developing girl coupled with a lack of joining seed. Fear of this situation would reflect the girl's disgust at her act of self-love. Nowadays, however, a myth can be seen as being of questionable value in the analysis of cases such as this. My thoughts, on witnessing Bess's dislike of swans went immediately to the root cause of her unhappiness and sense of disturbance: the domestic scene.

It was widely known, before Mrs Plantain for health reasons found herself having to employ a housekeeper, that domestic arrangements at Forton Court were immaculate. Any speck of dirt was instantly noticed and removed. China and glassware were washed with infinite care. The heart, or particular focus, of the house was, as is so often the case with housewives or chatelaines obsessed beyond the normal with cleanliness and order, the linen cupboard. Here, doubtless, were counted and embroidered sheets – and of the best linen, as would befit Mrs Plantain's estimation of her position in the world. Here also must be pillows – stuffed with the finest swansdown.

It was as difficult for Bess to accept my reading of her antipathy to swans as it would in all probability have been to try to persuade Mrs Plantain that her new housekeeper had proved to be as exhaustive and conscientious in her tasks as her mistress had been. After a succession of vehement 'Noes' – which are as revealing of the suppression of truth as the fiddling with an ornament at the neck – Bess admitted to a swansdown pillow – to the room, normally kept locked, where she had seen her father and Mrs Strang on an afternoon Mr Plantain had claimed he was due to drive to a distant farm – to a rump (and here my patient was overcome by embarrassment, but was helped to calm down and continue) propped up on this pillow and vigorously penetrated by her father, as particles of swansdown escaped and flew about.

Seventeen

As Bess crosses the floor of the quarry, after standing and looking out, there is movement – but very slight, almost inaudible, like shadows in an amphitheatre after players and spectators have gone home, like fleeing mice or like a piece of grit that has lodged in the eye, making double vision, blowing two leaves instead of one across an empty space. The twins are running, grey midgets in the

limestone shelves. They could be carrying ropes in-
finitesimally thin, to bind down their captive giants.

Jane, asleep at the quarry top, is easy to move. The
twins tie her arms with school scarves, grey and
knitted, stretched out until they are thin enough to
choke. They carry her down to the base of the
quarry, they blindfold and gag her with handker-
chiefs, and they wake Melanie – flat out by the
embers of the fire – when they see she is sleeping
with her head on the bag that contains the thermos,
and there is no way they can rob her of it without her
waking.

'What?' Melanie blinks at the two round heads
and four round eyes, the short, warm breath coming
down on her face.

'You're going somewhere better. Come on, we'll
show you.'

'Somewhere better?' Melanie, when she does
sleep, is slow to wake up.

'Up there.' Mary's index finger goes up, then
Mathilda's, like migrating cranes.

'Up there, at the top. There's water – in a sort of
tank – just over the top.'

'Water?' Melanie feels a sudden thirst. The last
Coke and Fanta went hours before: the sea, hundreds of feet below, makes the sound of a dry
tongue, rasping against the roof of a mouth.

'We've got some Opal Fruits for you.'

Melanie stares in wonder at the extended packet. She
asks no questions. She rises, pulls the bag securely to
her side, and follows the mousy shadows of the

twins up the side of the quarry. Only when she pauses for breath and looks down does she see Jane, who is straight as a peg doll, head jerking in an effort to shake off the gag and blindfold, arms bound behind her back. Even Melanie is perturbed by the sight.

'What – ?'

The twins pause too, as if they have to pretend to be human, to need to catch breath halfway up the quarry face.

'She's our hostage,' Mary says.

'She isn't Bess's real sister, after all,' says Mathilda.

Melanie looks down, uncomfortable. 'Well I dunno . . .'

'The Wind Man.' Mary puts on the bright lucid voice of the very young. Perhaps she and Mathilda still believe in this kind of thing – but surely not: Melanie stares at them in doubt. Faces round and eager in the dim light look unblinkingly back.

'We'll be up near the water,' says Mary.

'And we'll tell the others what to do,' Mathilda says simply. 'King of the castle.'

'Queen of the castle,' says Mary. They both laugh.

Bess pulls herself slowly up, in the short, tufty grass by the side of the quarry. She stops sometimes and looks out to sea – but the moon has gone for good, the stars give a dull light, the sea no longer has a garden of dancing courtiers. The second time she stops, she hears the fall of a pebble, smells – she thinks – the sudden tang of the sole of a plimsoll, hears its soft scrape against the jagged interface.

'Who's there?'

Bess's own ledge is just over her head, by now. She turns, looks upward last of all. The twins' heads look down, identical as swallows.

'It's all right. Bess. It's only us.'

Obscurely, by the twins, Bess can see Melanie's cruder head.

'What are you doing there?'

'You see, Bess – ' Mary swings down and stands beside her, precarious, where Bess is waiting to go up.

'We're going to stay here. It's ours.'

Bess gives out anger, in swirling hair, an arm that goes forward as if to shake the twin by the shoulder.

'Get out of there at once.'

'Bess.' Mathilda has leant further out of her perch. 'We aren't going to, see? I mean – '

And Mary puts in, 'You wouldn't want anything to happen to your sister.'

'My sister?' For a moment, Bess hardly knows what this can mean. But it's Mary, who stands by her now, who has uttered the threat.

'If she is your sister,' says Mary, with a snigger.

Bess sees the darkness of anger, like blood, come up behind her eyes and blot the sea, the cliff half-hewn away for its stone, the white ghostly pit, conch-shaped, where they are lost for good. She feels thirst – intolerable, burning thirst. And in the haze she sees that Jane is at the quarry's base, bound and still, slumped in the exhaustion of failing to escape.

'She's our hostage,' Mathilda says from above. 'There's three of us and only one of you. Isn't that right, Melanie?'

Melanie grunts agreement. She hates Bess, but this evil is not what she had expected.

'If you don't leave and go down to the bottom, we'll kill her,' Mathilda says again, from above. Mary looks up fleetingly, as if for once her twin has surprised her, then adds:

'Yes. Go down, Bess. You can't untie her, I'm afraid, till morning.'

'We'll see you. And come down.'

Bess gazes down over the quarry. There is no sign of Nat, no sign of life from the cavern, where Class Four lie huddled, waiting for morning. She doesn't know, as she stumbles down the stone face to Jane, why she has obeyed so quickly and readily. It must be that the twins, with their neat, sharp, synchronised movements, make her a Gulliver, a victim of their threading glances and needle-sharp bones. And Melanie – with her odd, frightening presence . . .

Bess reaches Jane. She kneels by the bound figure, whispers comfort into ears bruised by a gag tied hard under the hair at the back.

Mary and Mathilda stand on the topmost ledge, waving.

'We'll bring you some water – '

'In the morning – '. Their voices came down. Then, silence.

Clinical Report on Bess Plantain (continued):

I have shown at length . . . at what an early age sexual attraction makes itself felt between parents and children, and I have explained that the legend of Oedipus is probably to be regarded as a poetical rendering of what is typical in these relations. Distinct traces are probably to be found in most people of an early partiality of this kind – on the part of a daughter for her father, or on the part of a son for his mother; but it must be assumed to be more intense from the very first in the case of those children whose constitution marks them down for a neurosis, who develop prematurely and have a craving for love.

I quote here from Sigmund Freud* in order to clarify, I hope, the baffling predicament in which Bess found herself after the discovery of her father's relationship with Mrs Strang. Even if she had only on the deepest level accepted the fact of her father's impotence – and this, as we remember, had accounted for the nervous cough and other symptoms – she had now very suddenly to accept the

Case Histories, *Vol. 1: Dora* and *Little Hans*, Penguin, London, 1977.

opposite: to see her father, in fact, as something of a satyr; and also, most importantly, as the betrayer of her mother. It needed little probing to ascertain that Bess, too, felt herself betrayed by Mr Plantain's unfaithfulness. I was surprised, none the less, to find that on Bess's next visit the nervous cough had entirely disappeared – this was not to last more than a week or so – and that she remarked on her own strength and vigour, as if she had thought she might never regain them.

I asked Bess why she thought the traumatic experience of finding her father and Mrs Strang in this compromising situation had restored her to health. She did not at once reply what was in her mind, but told me she had had a dream on the preceding night; and as Bess had never once reported a dream, had always slept so soundly, she said, that no dream was remembered, I pressed her to relate it to me in as much detail as she could muster.

Bess's Dream

Water was rising inside the house. I had somehow to get to a door – it was in the middle of the house somewhere – and open the door so the water could get out. I was fighting to leave my room, but suddenly I was free. I was in a very beautiful dress and I remember there were pearls sewn all over it. I felt very strong, and I walked to the door, which I found without difficulty, and opened it. The water all swirled away and the house was safe. I left the house on the back of a horse.

There seemed little doubt at the time – though subsequent events have proved, unfortunately, that I was not quick enough to comprehend the most important 'clue' in Bess's dream – that Bess, in seeing in her mind a swirl of water, of water furthermore dammed up and now insistent of escape, was dreaming of her father: her father's previous frustration, that is, and the necessity for him to seek release with Mrs Strang, who, living as she did on the other side of the door leading to the former servants' wing, was represented by the door in the dream. Bess's subsequent sense of strength, as she related it to me, was surely in her having gained possession of a secret (a piece of knowledge to be kept from her mother). Had I paid more attention to the details of Bess's dress, as described by the dreamer, I would doubtless have paused here; but it appeared to me at the time that Bess was richly attired and jewelled as a result of her feeling of liberation (from the tyranny of the mother, from a sense of impotence) and had perhaps even achieved equality with her, for a fine dress and jewels are more familiar to mothers than to their schoolgirl daughters.

Bess had two choices to make at this juncture. She had either to feel jealousy of Mrs Strang, on the discovery of her father's potency, or to feel superior both to her mother (who must have at an earlier time been the subject of similar attentions on the part of Mr Plantain) and to Mrs Strang together; and the most efficient way to achieve this sense of superiority (the preferred choice, as jealousy must always be the more humiliating of the two) was to assume the identity of the father, to identify with him, that is, as the only actor in this drama aware of the roles played by the other participants. The pearls on Bess's dress I interpreted as symbolic of pearls of wisdom: a 'wisdom' or knowledge which set her father apart and which gave him mastery over wife and Mrs Strang. It was evident that Bess had lost her nervous cough as a result of acquiring this knowledge (heretofore considered by Mr Plantain to belong exclusively to him). Just as her father was no longer 'pent-up' since his ability to find release from sexual tension, so Bess's cough vanished as suddenly as it had come.

Although treatment was broken off very shortly after this (before the occasion of the walk of Saturday October 17th), I felt satisfied that some of Bess's problems, at least, had been laid to rest by the clear exposition to her of her return to infantile feelings for her father in defence of 'Uncle's' advances; and that the marked strength of her identification with the father could be reasonably attributed to her acquiring the secret of her father's relationship with Mrs Strang. Bess agreed to an additional possibility, that of a desire to be desired by her father (if 'Uncle' had paid court to her as well as to Mrs Strang, why should not her father?) and that she had in all probability reverted to an infantile sexual passion for her father in order to bring this about. I was surprised, however, by her insistence on the beauty of Mrs Strang – she dwelt often and passionately on the blackness of Mrs Strang's hair and the whiteness of her hands. At my suggestion that her identification with her father was responsible for this physical admiration, Bess declined to agree, and this not with the vehemence which so frequently indicates a hidden opposite meaning. Nor would she admit to a buried jealousy in this matter – and again absolute sincerity appeared to be the case, for she was in no way interested in my description of herself as a defeated rival. It took some time to discover that further secrets lay below the surface in this case.

In the event of both Mr and Mrs Plantain going away at the same time, Bess and Jane were sent to stay in the old servants' wing, now mostly unfurnished and undecorated as far as the upper floor went, and converted to a comfortable housekeeper's flat on the ground floor for Mrs Strang. The sisters were separated, at their own request, Jane sleeping in a small room near the door leading to the main house, Bess actually in Mrs Strang's room.

It was in describing these visits to Mrs Strang that Bess began first to manifest symptoms of unease. Emphasising at first that her admiration for Mrs Strang was purely that: Mrs Strang was 'more beautiful' and 'more elegant' a woman than any other Bess had known (and here we must infer that Bess's mother was directly presented as an unsuccessful contestant), Bess came finally to admit that she had first experienced this admiration when noticing 'Uncle's' interest in the housekeeper. On these visits to Mrs Strang's flat she had frequently been sent to 'play with Jane' in the unused rooms upstairs while 'Uncle' visited Mrs Strang in the bedroom she and Bess shared. The fact that these visits went unreported and therefore presumably unremarked by Bess over a period of time was tantamount, I suggested, to a positive compliance on her part. I put forward, furthermore, the theory that Bess had only betrayed the couple to her father when she realised he had half-guessed the situation and was suffering under the strain of it.

Bess's furious denial soon proved me right. It appears that one afternoon shortly after she had told her father of 'Uncle' and Mrs Strang's liaison, and 'Uncle' had been sent from the house in disgrace, Bess went to the first (bedroom) floor of the main house and hid in the linen cupboard, staying there for as long as an hour and thinking herself alone on that floor. She had every reason, once again, to believe Mr Plantain had gone in the car to a distant farm. She swore that she did this in play: that she and Jane had decided on a game of hide-and-seek; and that she had lost sense of the time, when Jane failed to find her. Only repeated investigation revealed the truth.

Bess had 'known', at the level of the unconscious, of her father's jealousy of his wife's stepbrother and his interest in Mrs Strang. She had seen her father and Mrs Strang together. She had known, also, that the housekeeper would hardly keep a rendezvous in a bedroom without deciding to change the linen, when the tryst was over. For all her protestations of an innocent and childish game, Bess had gone to the linen cupboard as a spy, reckoning that she would here be most liable to catch her father and Mrs Strang, to see if her father's interest in Mrs Strang was continuing, as she supposed.

An hour was not too long to wait, in this endeavour. I asked Bess whether she had sat or stood in the cupboard and was told she had 'been sitting, of course, on the soft pillows'. It was thenceforward clear that Bess's participation in the act of adultery between her father and Mrs Strang had been greater than I had supposed. For Mrs Strang came twice to the cupboard in that house (and this information was extracted from Bess only with the greatest difficulty): on the first occasion she had reached in a hand and removed the swansdown pillow on which Bess (who had hidden herself in a corner) had just been sitting; on the second, the pillowcase, soiled, was thrown back in and the pillow after it.

Bess's identification with her father was thus a good deal easier to understand, after the incident of the swansdown pillow. While he had on the one hand, only just (symbolically) missed penetrating his daughter – a moment earlier she had been reclining on the pillow – it was in the same sense true to say that Bess's previous occupancy had given her possession of the pillow and thus (symbolically) of Mrs Strang. Bess finally confided that the scene she had witnessed between her father and Mrs Strang, where 'the feathers coming down looked as if it was snowing', had given her a feeling of power and release from tension, and that she was ready to concur with my analysis of this identification with her father as being the principal cause for her (unfortunately temporary) loss of nervous symptoms such as the cough. She agreed also that her dream departure from the house on a horse signified a sense of masculine power. It is only to be regretted, as I remarked earlier, that details of Bess's regalia in the dream were not more accurately interpreted: in these cases of an abruptly-interrupted treatment, such omissions are likely to occur.

Eighteen

DAWN. BESS HAS dragged Jane into the space in the quarry, where Class Four lie asleep in a pudding steam of breath and duffle and sneakers kicked off. She and Jane lie against each other – she has managed to pull away the gag and blindfold and release the tied hands – and now Bess, peering out below the headband of stone, sees the first light of dawn in a smear over the sea. She has given up trying to find the ill child in the huddle of bodies: she feels instead the jumps and twitches of Jane as she dreams and she looks at the dawn as if it could come down and rescue them all, pull them into its dim light and carry them home over the hills.

It's hardly worth going out again to watch the fog. It creeps nearer, hanging now only a few hundred yards from the broken basin of stone where the girls cling; the twins high up, near the rim, with Melanie asleep over her *Nature Notes*, the others, with Bess, in an indeterminate mess at the bottom. What's the sense, when the fog will come and take away even the dawn, the rags of light that might have saved them? The fog will fold in all the growing light in the sky in a wide, white gulp: it is perfectly light, the fog, but you can't see in it. Bess watches the sea, where soon they will be driven by the fog. They will walk under the water, until the fog comes down even over the sea and pumps the breath out of their lungs to join the white vapour. Since her act of surrender at the top of the quarry, the courtiers on the waves are quiet – except for a white stocking here, or the buckle of an abandoned shoe, in the sea. The Queen, quick to yield to her enemies, has returned the expanse of grey water to a heath.

Jane dreams, as Bess's thin, nervous cough shakes her so she jumps in her sleep. She dreams of the leagues she has to walk, by nightfall: then another day and night: then another, and more, until seven pairs of iron shoes are worn out. She has to wake the Prince, the Sleeping Beauty of a Prince, who has his rosebud mouth slightly open in sleep, in a round room at the top of the tower circled by roses. She can't get in to the tower, because what seemed to be a hedge of thorns – which she could easily have cut down – turns out to be a wrapping of coats, piles on piles of them, snugly fitting over the tower. No sooner does she find the buttons, than the coat peels away and there is another, with the Prince wrapped up somewhere inside. Jane's arms ache and twitch as she unbuttons – all to no avail. And when she gives up, to lie on a mossy bank at the foot of the tower, she feels the first happiness and rest she has known. A river flows at her feet. She pulls off the iron shoes. She is no longer Jane.

Melanie, in her look-out post high above the sea, has turned once to watch the fog as it creeps up so quietly you could never catch it moving. She has slept, and woken again and slept – but something about the twins makes her uncomfortable – they lie locked together, smug: she wants to break the puzzle. She opens *Nature Notes* and writes with the smart pen from the kiosk:

I am glad I was runin away when I did or I wudnt see Lorri who is my friend she let off the missl and the nukle war is started it is cumin then Lorri will take me in the boat an we leave

Melanie pauses, looks out at the dawn, the shreds of light that are filling blood red in the sun. Another warm, beautiful day, in this Indian summer – she has heard Bess and Jane's mother talk like that, on the September day she was summoned by the silly tall man, Jane and Bess's 'Uncle', for a game of hide-and-seek with the other village children, at Forton Court. Melanie had had to go right through the sitting-room – and Mrs Plantain had merely waved, told her to find the girls upstairs, that the game had already started.

Bess's room is daft an she was cros wen I cum in she got posh posters bally an ponys an a Queen an she was all dresst up wen she tole me get out I went down the pasige an then there was the door open I thot it was a toilet but it had sheets Lorri an the tall man was kissing but I still lov Lorri

'Another warm, beautiful day in this Indian summer we're having,' Bess's mother had said again when Melanie came down. And, 'Did you find Jane?'

Melanie giggles, thinking of Jane makes her look down at the cavern under the shelf: it serves Bess and Jane right to have been made to go there. Then she frowns, as she swivels in her high throne and gazes at the beach where Laurie is waiting for her to come. She thinks – I'll get them twins to fill that thing up with water an I'll take it down now – when she sees figures on the beach: either two or three, it's too far to make out clearly. Melanie mutters and drops her pen. It bounces down the quarry, but silently, taking no stones with it. Melanie rises, bumps her head against the side of the cliff. If it was Bess – and Jane – creeping down to the boat, making an escape from the fog, leaving them all prisoners . . . Or if it was someone's Dad – not hers anyway – come to catch her, to put her back home . . .

It is important not to be seen. Melanie pulls herself up on to the cliff and walks inland, looking for a path to go down. She has the thermos with her, in the carrier bag from the kiosk; she passes the drum where rainwater has collected and fills it slowly and adroitly; and she glances only once at the thick bandage of coiling fog before stepping into its folds and groping for the way down.

Nineteen

NAT HAD FOUND the boat too heavy to move – after pushing, on wet stones black from the spray, and feeling its heaviness, after scraping her shoulder and bruising her knees against the battered sides of the boat – she had climbed in, defeated, and lay until first light under the narrow seat in the prow. It was cold, by the sea, where the wind that had left the quarry still came in darts and gusts. But the wind, at least, made a bank of white foam out to sea: it made a ridge, of intangible shingle, of white spray pebbles melting and forming. Nat could think, as she crouched, eyes closed, on the damp-spotted boards, that she was on the beach where her father had gone and where he was bound to return.

At dawn the cold and wet had become unbearable. Nat climbed out of the boat and stood stamping her feet on the stones. Her sneakers slipped on the round, large stones and her feet squeezed between them, the stones nudged her ankles and gripped hard before letting go. Nat cried, as she hadn't at home for a long time. Thirst pinched her throat, salt water ran on her cheeks and into her mouth, the salty spray of the sea blew in her eyes and down her face again.

Dawn made a straggling flight of white clouds in the sky. The clouds vanished into night. Then more came. They massed over the sea, in a dull white bank, over the watery bank of the waves out to sea. Nat saw the two ridges, two strips of white stones thrown up by the sea to protect itself from the big swell beyond. Her tears merged them, made a white arc, a sea-bow. Sea and sky were joined in a circle.

Nat's father flew and floated in the radiant circle of cloud and spray. His arms were stretched out, he was coming nearer. Nat ran, falling, over the stones to the edge of the sea.

The first Chesil Bank went, in a spit of bubbles, as the wind raced off to the south. The sea heaved, grey. The second bank widened in the sky. A white, flat morning came down.

Nat waded in, until the water came up to her knees. There was something there, all the same – it was lying on the water – Nat couldn't see her father's face, and she wondered that his arms were so wide and long. It wasn't moving, except with the sea: but the waves edged it to the stones. Then, as Nat went back, and her feet danced without holding, and she fell, half in and half out of the water, the rough feel of it dangled for a moment at her neck. It was a rough embrace, indifferent, shoved up by the sea. Wet feathers, white once, now grey and streaked, water slapping over a broken wing.

Melanie has found the path: the fog has held back, even, as if shrinking from her first visit. She has no fear, the path was secure under her feet, she is already on the black stones, ready to prevent escape, or rescue Laurie, or overturn boulders and throw them at the enemy. Some of the strength that comes when there are nights of disturbance at home, makes her march over the slippery backs of the stones without falling. She looks ahead – at the sea, at Laurie's cave in a blur, where the white boulder is still in place. At first, seeing only what could be a head in the water and a wing perhaps at a sinking angle, she stops in her tracks and stares. The stone under her feet rocks and she is propelled onwards – to the sea monster, the human-headed bird pushed on to the beach by the waves. She almost runs – it's as if the stones are tilting her down into the sea – and only when she is in danger of falling headlong, on stones that have their base in the seabed and are still wet at the bottom, sticking up as far as low tide will let them go – does she throw her arms out and stop. She laughs and calls: 'Nat!' She stretches out a hand, seeing already the feast she will have with Laurie – Nat can come too, if she likes – the fire lit with the kiosk lighter, the fresh water drunk from the neat cup at the top of the thermos, and the succulent, roasted swan.

Twenty

IT's NEVER EASY to say why one incident rather than another should trigger off a sequence of events: in this case, however, we can only assume, on the evidence of Bess's analysis, that swans had come to play an important part in the child's inner emotional life. Bess connected the powerful bird with the realisation of her father's sexuality and adultery – and, as Dr Ross informed us, also with death, for when asked by him to describe her vision of the probable end of humankind, she replied that the bomb was 'like a great swan's egg, that would explode and wipe out the world with its gas'. She associated the bird, too, with pride and with 'thinking too much of yourself', but this feeling of guilt may have been caused more by the embarrassment of having to undergo what was (clearly even to her) a form of treatment of questionable worth in the modern age, a treatment more suited to individuals before the first world war of this century than to a young girl of the second generation of nuclear disaster, daughter of an age, too, of chemical answers to emotional problems. Bess's shame at identifying with the swan is therefore twofold: a blithe arrogance is implied, a narcissism, a failure to understand that the threat now is to the whole human race, that the time for preening, for reflections is past; and shame at the swan as symbol of her father's potency, her guilty complicity and taking-over of the mantle of her father's power. These are the underlying reasons, we presume (or some of them at least) for Bess's sudden step away from reality over that hairline skipped across daily by all children (who are then drawn back again to the intransigence of the adult world). The extreme situation must also, of course, be taken into account: a colony of girls, hungry and thirsty in a hole in the rock over the sea. The fog, the 'naughtiness' of the children a few years younger, a naughtiness that could be seen as crime, as evil intentions. And the sense of loss of control, with an army of infants ready to rebel and one of them already lying like dead. At any rate, we can see Bess's reactions more clearly if we take these factors into account – if we watch her cross the quarry and look down the narrow path to the cave where Laurie sits hidden behind her white boulder – see her stare down at the beach where Melanie and Nat struggle together with the body of a swan – hear her in-drawn breath as the long, still-beautiful bird is dragged over the black stones to the curving path upward to Laurie's cave. We see Bess turn like a general on her heel. There is something inevitable in her measured pace down the side of the cliff. The sea's greyness makes a quiet, a waiting for her proclamation. She walks with head high, the whitening dawn in a ruff at her neck. She rounds the last bend to the cave.

Melanie has pulled the boulder aside, in her excite-ment at presenting the gift. Laurie leans, half-kneeling, against the wall of the cave. She is as pale as an anchorite. The cave smells musty. Nat climbs up behind Melanie, the tail of the great bird in her arms. Melanie half-stumbles, pushing forward the orange beak, the only stripe of colour in the leaden hand of the day.

'It's for a feast, Laurie! Here!'

Laurie hardly looks up. She might see the be-draggled feathers of the swan out of the corner of her eye, or she might think she is dreaming, for she pulls listlessly at hair fallen across her face. Melanie pushes in even nearer. 'Look, Laurie, please. It's a surprise, it's for you!'

Bess, slow on the path, reaches the cave. She has

pulled off her sweater and the white ruff of the shirt meets the white dawn at her neck. The twins, who have been spying from the quarry, come down and stand behind her in silent awe. For the twins can sense power – their father has taught them that power is all – and Bess has it now.

Nat and Melanie see Bess only when they hear her voice, loud and cold in the absence of sound from the sea. They look up – they see the red hair – thin lips – a face sharp and commanding.

'You give that swan to me. You follow me and you obey my orders. Swans are the property of the Queen!'

The Journal of Laurence Lelandes

As I sit here, in this cave in the rock with the white stone, I hear my mother's voice in the sea. I have to climb down to get back to her, and as I go I feel my legs and arms fall away, in the last slither, in the air thick with salt. I have to go back.

But my mother is high up in the house, shaking out the sheets. Since we came here it is always sheets – are they always soiled, in Monsieur's house? – Madame is so clean it's like a crust round her, Madame's younger brother gives off a perfumed smell – yet my mother piles the sheets and counts them, stacks them in bales, in fields of flax. Always the best linen sheets here for Madame. My mother piles them in the dark closet at the end of the carpeted lane. Do I smell something sweet, as if sugar had been poured in the sea?

Where we were before, the sheets were threadbare and you could look out through them at the fresh fields and where they were darned a yellow glow of buttercups. You could always see straight ahead, in the stiff rooms where there was nothing to fall over. Here, there are tricks and traps. My mother went away and another woman came to take her place. I wear the white sheet, the white mourning of the court.

As I sit here, I see my sister and my enemy, coming to pull me away from the sea. We exchanged rings, we wrote our mottoes on the stable wall: *Semper eadem* for her, always the same, she's a rock, or a stone; *semper mutata resurgam* was mine. I come back always in a different shape, or guise, daughter of the Guise, queen from France, her sister and her enemy. How flirtatious she is! I stay wrapped in white, while she pulls on glitter, gold leather belts that look as if an icon had poured off its gold to please her. Her red hair is dusted gold, too. Her lips are thin and a cruel red, like holly berries. She leads the way, I follow.

You know the dark closet at the end of the passage. It was her idea of a game. It's hide-and-seek, an

English children's game Madame's brother likes to play. Oh let's have the children in from the village, he says, let's play hide-and-seek. You know how long you can hide, in hide-and-seek. You can hide for centuries, under beds that sat centuries there, in a smell of blanket you can lie asleep until the rough prickle wakes you.

Madame looks cross. The woman who is no longer my mother has a curly smile like a worm going across her face. Madame doesn't like it when the house is filled with the voices of children. The stamping feet make her see mud and mess, the house going down into the fields it came up from. The woman who is not my mother keeps her smile as she goes to the closet and unfolds, folds up, resettles all the sheets.

What about Monsieur? He doesn't want to be left out of this. But he would lose his dignity, if he crept under his own beds, surprised his own ghosts behind the curtains. He has to sit downstairs with Madame, and listen to the thump of the house, the hiding and running that sends the house halfways over like a lurching boat, the seeking that can empty the house entirely, with a long shriek going right out into the hall. He has to watch, in his agony, the slow summer light fade in the garden, over beds of blue flowers. Little hot flies from the summer night come to tease his face, to dance on the lamps as Madame turns them on and says it's dinner-time. When will this game end? When will the children go home? Where are Mrs Strang's daughter and Madame's younger brother? And Monsieur thinks of the dark closet, where he can't go now, for fear of finding what he had thrown in himself, from when he had been lying in the sheets.

I have to go back to my mother. I can start at the top of the house, and swing over the banisters, down. I know the suffocating pool of the stairs, the water waiting. But before I reach her I always wake, by the dark closet at the end of the red-carpeted lane, where the game is playing and drawing me in. A hand comes out, and draws me in.

Twenty-one

SUN SHINES BUT under it there is cold, the cold of winter that is coming down any day now. And the fog, the cold white fog has edged nearer like the uninvited dragon at the feast, puffing out its white breath at the girls as they sit eating. Forks of fire shoot up at the fog, which seems to melt lazily round them, to agree to disappear and then to form again.

The swan is roasted, the meat is running with fat. The fingers of Class Four are shiny with fat. There is water from the drum on the top of the cliff. The blue sky directly above, embroidered with woolly white clouds, sits down over the group like a child's cardigan.

The ill child lies still in the cavern under the ledge. And Laurie has refused to join the feast. These are the two considerations for Bess, Queen of the cliffs, the hollowed-out rock, the stones. Already the ill child has been dismissed as dead by her classmates.

'She doesn't do nothing if you pinch. Look!' Before being pulled away, the most vigorous of the nurses in Class Four has demonstrated the child's lifelessness. And it's true, Bess can't tell if she breathes or not. At one time, the chest seemed to give out breath – but it could have been like listening to the sea, to a shell held to the ear, an imagined murmuring. Melanie has assured Bess that the child is perfectly well.

'She's always stayin' back from school, Miss.' (Melanie, anxious to show that she respects Bess's new power, is unsure of the form of address.) 'Always got a cold or a sniffle or somethin', Miss.'

But they are eating, the sun comes on them with its hint of ice, they can't think of the ill child now. Laurie and her absence are more of an irritant: why can't the girl come when she's told?

Melanie has her answers to this, of course. She bows, she smiles and fawns at Bess, as soon as Class Four starts to mutter 'Thank-you Your Majesty' at the offer of more roast swan, she is eager to join in. But she knows who holds the real power here. A small cave, a court with as yet only one member – but a Queen who can control the white fog, the gas of the end of the world, with her white missal, is waiting there now to assume her rightful place. Later, Melanie will take her scraps of swan, and water – and courtiers, servants loyal and devoted to her cause. She will reassure the pale figure, who sits on in the cave, the white boulder drawn across once more. Armies will rise up, to throw Bess from her throne and restore the French, Catholic Queen.

Not that Melanie knows much of history. She has heard of Good Queen Bess – and always hated the pictures in the book at school, the posh bitch looked like she was trying to be Prime Minister; and she's heard of the poor Scotch Queen who came over from France and got her head cut off. And she's seen Bess and Laurie playing, of course, when she's been up to the Big House for hide-and-seek and seen them in gold and black – or white, usually for Laurie, curtseying – posing when they're not in fits of giggles. And it's in the Chamber of Horrors, where they went on the school outing and Melanie's mother never gave in the £2.50 for the trip, so there was a row. A very pale neck, and blood on the block, and an axe that looks like it's been falling hundreds of years and could never get there, to sever the neck. She's the talk of time, the Queen who lost her head. Melanie knows she has come back to demand retribution and to receive it. Those who love her, fight on her side, will be saved from the deathly fog.

Twenty-two

WHO WILL MELANIE take first, for her loyal troops? As Bess, smiling and confident, red hair bright as a sovereign in the sun – cough gone, health restored – sits unknowing on her makeshift throne above the cavern of the populace, Class Four, Melanie leaves the feast and wanders to the ledge where the twins are now settled. It's been edifying, the sudden conversion of the twins to Bess's cause after their impudent binding up of Jane the night before: they know power when they see it, Melanie decides. Bess's change of demeanour has impressed them. They will follow her – into battle, out of danger, away from the creeping fog. They must be split, Melanie sees, divided and weak. If she can't get the two of them to join Laurie's forces, then they must fight each other. Besides, Melanie doesn't like the sufficiency of their two selves: it's time the smug smiles went and they were lost, like her, like the rest of humanity, searching for the lost part which can never be found. Melanie swings up to the ledge with the assurance of an emissary, and settles beside them.

'What d'you want?' Mary squints down at Melanie. This isn't a good opening: Melanie remembers, with discomfort, that it's said that twins have psychic powers. They know her plan. But then – hasn't she got something special herself? She thinks of the heavy cupboards shifting in the cramped room at home, the falling plates, and she braces herself. A silence can be menacing. So she stays where she is, without making a move. The twins pay no attention. They are playing chess on the miniature board. Some rejected scraps of swan's meat lie beside them on the stone ledge.

'You aren't really the same, you know.' This is Melanie's opening gambit. It is said casually. She picks up a shred of swan's skin and nibbles at it, as if she had dropped in at their invitation, had brought up a subject worthy of debate. The twins don't answer, Mathilda is moving a pawn up the board.

'No one's the same anyway. What your dad says is balls, my dad says.'

At this Mary looks up. Her father the teacher is often attacked for being an 'extremist': it's hard to know quite what is meant. But direct attacks such as this one are rare.

' 'E says everyone's the same. My dad says tell that to the madams.' Melanie paused; this doesn't sound quite right. However, she is getting a rise.

Mathilda has looked up too, and Mary holds a miniature rook aloft – looking down at the small board again it's clear she has forgotten where she was going to place it.

'As for you two, ev'ryone knows what the difference is,' Melanie giggles. All the same, her heart is beginning to thump: this is dangerous ground.

'And what is that?' Mary speaks quietly, puts the rook down at the edge of the board.

'Don't let's pay any attention.' Mathilda hands her back the piece. 'Let's get on with the game.'

'Difference *is* the game,' says Melanie. Another giggle, but a hollow one. Because, by now, four round, hostile eyes are staring straight at her. 'Mary always wins.'

This time the silence comes from the twins and Melanie is frightened by it. She longs to look down over the ledge, to see how far there is to fall if she should be pushed. But she knows this would be fatal, and sits frozen in her apparently casual pose.

'Who says?' This is Mathilda, as low and quiet as her twin.

'Mary does, silly. She tells ev'ryone in the playground. I 'eard her, ev'ryone 'eard 'er. She's cleverer so she can't be the same, got it?'

The twins rise. The chess board goes under Mathilda's heel. Suddenly, as if she had been calculating the move all along, Melanie swings down from the ledge and runs to the feast. Bess looks surprised, stretches out an arm as if to ward her off.

'What's happening, Melanie?'

'It's Mary and Mathilda. They're fighting, Your Majesty.'

'Fighting?' Bess stares up in apprehension at the ledge. 'But they never fight, surely?'

Melanie hisses, delighted – for the twins are indeed wrestling on the ledge – and they look babyish, Melanie thinks, when normally they're like little old people, with their science and their chess. Bess calls out in anger. The twins hear and stop. But not before Class Four has witnessed this strange outbreak: two or three start to cry.

'I wanna go 'ome.'

'Wot they fightin' for?'

'It's the Wind Man making them.'

Melanie grins. They've pretty well got it right. She is as fleet as the Wind Man, she can leap like Peter Pan, only better than that crappy one on old wires in the village hall, she can serve her cause and her Queen. She turns away as the twins come down from their ledge, to report to Queen Bess and explain their actions as best they can. She goes over to find Jane, who is right at the edge of the quarry, looking out to sea. Yet, as she draws near, even Melanie finds she must slow her step. Something has happened to Jane – the back view shows it – she is standing so straight, her shoulders are square, different – for a moment Melanie wonders if the Wind Man really did come and change her: not in the cradle, though, but last night. She can hardly be asked to stand against her own sister – unless, of course, she really believes that Bess has never been her sister at all. Melanie can't help taking another step or two, at the thought of the cleverness of her manoeuvres. Surely, Jane will be happy to join Laurie the true Queen; and there will be one of the twins; and Nat, who will scarcely notice what's happening at all, can be persuaded there are better dreams to be had with Laurie than with Bess. Melanie has few doubts about her ability to win over Class Four. Her army will conquer effortlessly. In her last second before tapping Jane on the back, in this Grandmother's Footsteps with only Melanie aware of the rules, she feels a surge of the power that used to come in the 'disturbances' at home. The light thickens and whitens a little, her last step is unsteady. But it is with a surprisingly light hand that she raps on Jane's back. Jane swings round. She looks as if she is expecting something, but not this.

'Jane – ' Melanie falters, but this is a clever step too. Jane has to speak first, to appear to be asking Melanie a question. At first, she keeps her mouth shut; then irritation at Melanie intruding – ugly, clumsy Melanie with the fat cheeks and the white circles in the fat under the eyes – forces her to snap out the question.

'What d'you want?'

'Come with me to take food to Laurie,' Melanie has a weak, supplicating tone.

'Food to Laurie?'

'Bess is wicked. She wouldn't let me take the meat to her. Bess is the wicked Queen.' Now Melanie speaks in the high 'elocution' voice they teach at

132

school for drama. 'Queen Laurie is the rightful Queen.' Jane's eyebrows rise in astonishment and Melanie rushes on, her self again: 'She 'asn't 'ad warter or anythin', it's terrible you know Bess is tryin' to kill 'er an' she's got the missle for the nukle war an' she made this fog an' everythin'.'

'What?' Jane backs, sees she's at the edge of the cliff, and stops. The mad girl is going to push her over, is trying to poison her, the girl who hangs round her at school until she could kick her away, who piles in on top of her at hide-and-seek when there's a big game at Forton Court, who breathes her Mars Bar breath down her neck in the crush behind the curtains, under the bed – this fat girl from the Whitehays Estate who said she was really Jane and Jane was she, is trying to turn her against her own sister, to threaten her otherwise with a sea plunge, a dash against the rocks.

So Jane steps forward. For all that, something has changed in her since they all set off with the Walks Woman to the Mapperton tree. She is strong, her will is unbounded, yet it has no direction: she has no idea who she may turn out to be. Only her instinct will show her; and her instinct makes her strike Melanie in the chest, so that she staggers back, with a hoarse grunt as if her wind had been knocked out of her. Jane still has a straight walk and square shoulders as she sidesteps and heads inland, for the embers of the fire and Bess directing Class Four to collect the leftovers of swan and load them into a carrier bag from the kiosk. She looks back only once, to give a derisive laugh, to point up at the sky over the quarry, the sky inland clear now with only a few clouds and even a chilly pale blue emerging.

'She couldn't keep her special fog, though, could she?' Jane speaks clearly, the fear in her breath has gone.

Melanie gazes into the sky. Her mouth does a cartoon droop. But – although the fog has gone, blown by the wind, capricious as Dorset sea mists tend to be, heavy and choking one moment, drifting, dancing off the next – although the others look up, following Jane's hand and see it gone – it is too late to set off for home. The girls are securely caught in the web of their own weaving, and the filaments are clouded over, like a web that gorged on the mist.

Twenty-three

BESS SEES THE departing fog, and decides she will make up her mind later on the best course of action. The warmth from the sun, and the roasted swan's meat, and the waves that go on rolling, and disappearing, and rolling up again, have made her drowsy and royal, a Queen of Hearts half asleep on her ledge, secure in her power and role. She can't see the grass at Forton Court – or her room wrapped in its tight trellis paper, or school – she hardly cares, even, that the sulky girl in the cave by the sea has disobeyed her command to attend the feast. She sees the waves, and the sprays of lace and ruff and frills that rise and fall in the dance of courtiers, as they make obeisance to her throne. The sun hangs over her wrist, a round gold orb.

Bess has no idea either of Melanie's plans or of Jane's weightless state. She expects them as much as the others to do her bidding – perhaps to go out before dark to chase some other wild animal for the evening meal, to sing the songs she likes the court to sing. She has no inkling of what has caused the twins to fight for the first time in their identical lives – but as they said they were sorry, and felt sick because they'd eaten too much too quickly – she granted them a pardon and allowed them to return to their ledge. Bess might have divined, by the sight of a tiny rook, plastic and deformed by a stamping heel, which has fallen from above and lies by her hand on the ledge, that all is not well above. In the household of economy run by the twins' father, a chess set is not easily thrown away. And the twins are famous for their patience and determination over the game. Bess might have seen, in the trodden-over board and bishops and queens lying in disarray, the approaching insurrection.

Nevertheless, some instinct of self-preservation causes her to look down at the rabble in the cavern under the ledge where she has installed herself so regally. There have been cries and shouts there all afternoon – at one point two of them came out brandishing forked sticks, as if they meant to attack – and the problem of the ill child must be solved. It might be typhus, or even the plague, contracted up at the Posy Tree in some magical contagion of disease and time. Fever might break out, forcing a removal of the court. Bess swings her legs down on to the uneven stone of the quarry floor and stoops to enter the plebeian hole.

This is not the only reason why a visit to Class Four seems timely. Bess has seen Jane, at the edge of the quarry, turn and stand face to face with Melanie. She has seen her own sister, usually so 'old for her age', punch Melanie in the chest. Even if the tension of their circumstances, the fear of being lost in a sea-fog without food or shelter, can be held responsible for this behaviour, as much as for the outbreak of hostilities between the twins, Bess is in no mood for giving out further reprimands. And she can't under-stand the look on Jane's face – she has never seen it before – as Jane strides on, in her tights and sweater like a young page, to the centre of the keep, where the fire still smoulders after the feast. Bess ducks under the ledge, into the tweaking hands and shov-ing elbows of Class Four.

Just what might be expected. Gasps, popping eyes at the vision of Bess descended among them. And the news – she had expected this too.

'Can we 'ave a spade, Your Majesty?'

'We're gonna bury 'er at the top of the cliff there,

can we 'ave crayons to colour a stone on the place?'
'Like when my tortoise died.'

Bess goes over to the inanimate figure of the child. She turns, snappy schoolmarm voice, to push away the jostling crowd.

'How on earth do you think I have spades and crayons here? Are you all out of your minds?'

Silence. Bess now has time to bend over the child. She sees – the cheeks are very pale – but the spots are gone. It's possible – Bess bends down – just possible – she blows out softly, on to the child's face. Yes, the nostrils quiver. Then a flutter at the eyelashes. The silence grows heavier in the cave, where the air is thick with sniffles and over-breathed air.

'Make a path.' Bess's tone is imperious. 'At once.'

A winding path is made, between knees filthy over stained socks. Bess half-drags, half-walks the ill child to the entrance to the cavern. She pulls her outside, to the late, gold sun. She stands her upright. The child's eyes open. A murmur runs through Class Four.

'She made 'er breathe.'
'She done it. Bess.'
'The Queen.'

The ill child has spots of colour now in her cheeks, she takes a step and sits down abruptly on Bess's ledge. With royal magnanimity Bess makes her more comfortable, winds a cardigan at her neck. Class Four starts to chatter in excitement – as Jane strolls up from one corner and Melanie from the path that leads down to the sea. Jane arrives first. She smiles at her sister – but her look is still strange.

'That's wonderful,' she says.

Bess nods, self-deprecating, knowing really that her divine touch can hardly have been the reason for the child's recovery, yet half-believing it all the same. Melanie walks up, as the twins drop from their ledge to see what makes the monkey chatter of Class Four. Ignoring them, Melanie turns to Bess with a sickly smile.

'Laurie got a man with 'er now, down there.'

Clinical Report on Bess Plantain (continued):

It is only after the events succeeding the Walk of Saturday October 17th that I am able to look back over the (interrupted) treatment of Bess Plantain and add various notes which seemed less relevant at the time than they do now. In due course, I hope to see the patient again: at present I am advised that extreme shock has rendered any form of communication impossible.

As I remarked before, it was clear that a web of jealousy, love and hatred lay beneath the calm and stoical façade which Bess presented to the world. I was sure, too, that the temporary alleviation of nervous symptoms was due to the identification with the father after the discovery of her father's liaison with Mrs Strang. What I had not sufficiently taken into account, however, was the extent of transference in this case: that practically every player of a part in Bess's emotional drama could be and was replaced by another, at some point: that Bess herself had little or no control over the roles the recipients of her affections would next be expected to play; and that a second drama, as powerfully 'real' as the one concerning human relationships, was also in the process of being acted out.

The first clue, on re-reading the files of the case, comes in Bess's continued emphasis on the beauty, 'black hair' and 'very white hands' of her father's mistress, Mrs Strang. As Bess was accustomed to sleep in Mrs Strang's bedroom on the occasion of her parents' absence from Forton Court, I translated this strong feeling of aesthetic admiration as a genuine transference: while her father was away, the daughter could 'pay court' to Mrs Strang, which would include complimentary remarks on her appearance. It has not become clear to me until now, however, that Mrs Strang was an unlikely possessor of very white hands: she was, as Bess often told me, continually washing 'and with her arms up to her elbows in the sink': whether she protected her hands or not, the continual housework expected of her by Mrs Plantain (and indeed her own standards were extremely high) made it probable that her hands would show the mark of it. (For this *aperçu* I must thank my wife, with whom I have discussed the case since the events of the Walk.) It became my duty, therefore, to discover the identity of the individual for whom Mrs Strang was, so to speak, standing in. It was not necessary to look far. Mrs Strang's twelve-year-old daughter, never mentioned by Bess in any of her sessions with me, was the obvious choice. I regret the fact that I did not question Bess more closely as to the exact number of people living at Forton Court at the time: as I commented earlier, this case, already showing so highly significant a number of transference examples, seemed complete without the addition of another actress to the list.

This actress, it must be stated, has claims to being the principal all along (not, of course, that this obviates the accuracy of the diagnoses of the patient's relationships with her father, her mother and 'Uncle'). It was on to her that Bess poured her displaced feelings, and here I again feel that it will be of use to quote Sigmund Freud:

> It has long been known and often been pointed out that at the age of puberty boys and girls show clear signs, even in normal cases, of an existence of an affection for people of their own sex. A romantic and sentimental friendship with one of her schoolfriends, accompanied by vows, kisses, promises of eternal correspondence, and all the sensibility of jealousy, is the common precursor of a girl's first serious passion for a man. Thence-

forward, in favourable circumstances, the homosexual current of feelings often runs completely
dry . . . When, in a hysterical woman or girl, the
sexual libido which is directed towards men has
been energetically suppressed, it will regularly be
found that the libido which is directed towards
women has become vicariously reinforced and
even to some extent conscious . . .

It would be difficult to predict now that the circumstances of Bess Plantain will be favourable, or
even that they have a chance of being so. The
disastrous events on the Isle of Portland will en-
hance, I very much fear, the homosexual tendency:
as soon as Bess is able to resume treatment, I shall of
course concentrate on the task of eliminating this
undesirable tendency, however low the odds that I
will eventually succeed.

Bess and Mrs Strang's daughter, Laurence, it now
appears, were inseparable. Her name must be added
to that of the patient wherever Bess claims she was
alone; and this must include the fateful linen cupboard where the swansdown pillows and pillow-
cases were kept. A clearer picture begins to emerge
when we see that Bess refers to this cupboard and to
hide-and-seek in the same breath; when we connect
a strong emotion of jealousy with Bess's feelings
towards the girl; and the repression which had been
effected for her feelings for her father.

Only a further interview with the patient will determine what actually took place in the linen cupboard, thus prompting what was clearly intended to be one death on the tragic occasion of the Isle of Portland and which turned out, just as tragically, to be another. But it would be reasonable to suppose that the libidinous 'Uncle', having seduced Mrs Strang and made an unsuccessful bid for the patient herself, had gone on to make love to the housekeeper's daughter; and this on the occasion of a game of hide-and-seek, and in the linen cupboard which has played so important a part in our investigations.

For the present, I can only return to the revising of my thoughts at the time, however, and, late though it is, make further notes on the significance of the rich and regal attire worn by Bess in her dream. For this attire points to the existence of the second and 'costume' drama which was in the process of being acted out by these young women.

It is possible that further research will tell us more of the last stages of development, prior to the onset of the menses in pre-pubertal girls, when a glamorised view of history, of queens and kings and their passions (and often tragic destinies) becomes obsessional to a degree quite unknown at any other time in life.

Twenty-four

MELANIE HAD GONE down the path to the cave with a paper napkin, part of the plunder from the kiosk, filled with scraps of roasted swan; her thermos was filled with water, slightly rusty-looking now as the container at the top of the cliff began to empty. There was no answer from behind the boulder, when she called and knocked – and for a time she stood uncertain, staring down at the black stones on the beach, and the sea that ran in and out of them like water in broken plates. If Laurie had left, pulling aside the white boulder and seeing a clear sky, fog gone, the world of schools and exercise books and the twins' father standing by the blackboard at Melplash Comprehensive – if Laurie had disappeared, then Melanie would go too, even to the home she had run away from for ever, even to the rage of her parents and the moods and the light that changed when they came on and the things hurled terrifyingly across the room. She would leave mad Bess and this group of girls infected by her madness, stuck like flies on the edge of a crevasse. With Laurie she would walk back to the village in the folds of the hills, on an ordinary autumn afternoon, with the leaves just turning. There might even be conkers. Melanie found herself hoping, even with the return home ahead, that this could be true. Yet she knew, before the slight movement inside the cave became a flutter of a hand, before the boulder shifted cautiously on its pebbly base, that Laurie would not have had the strength to walk home alone. She had had nothing to eat or drink since the beginning of the expedition. Her expression was strange and she was pale. Melanie knew the thin, very white hand would come out, extended in love again for the only true friend she had.

'I've brought you some swan.'

The hand was drawn in again. Melanie frowned. She shoved her head against the side of the boulder as if she wanted to butt it out of position.

'And the fog's gone. Was it you done it, Laurie? You taken it away, what for?'

Slowly, the boulder was pulled back again; Laurie had retreated. Melanie felt bewilderment, then anger. All the same, she placed the paper napkin carefully on the ledge outside the entrance to the cave. When Laurie wanted it, no doubt – Laurie knew best. Yet a faint doubt, more painful than actual pain, crept into her mind. Suppose Laurie didn't care for her at all? Suppose, as well, it was Bess who was really the strong one here: the fog had gone of its own accord and was nothing to do with the white book, the stupid white book Laurie sat with all day in the cave: Bess was leader and Laurie would easily be crushed by her – suppose the twins, who were famed for being in the right place at the right time, had been right again this time, quickly abandoning their tricks on Bess and Jane when they saw where the real power lay? It all seemed horribly possible. Melanie straightened, then applied her eye to the crack between cave and boulder for one last look at her heroine. Surely, one glance at that exquisite face would prove all these doubts worthless? It was with the eager devotion of a worshipper at Lourdes that Melanie strained to gaze in at the French girl (as she was known in the village) – the martyr, the Catholic Queen.

It was very dark inside the cave. Melanie felt the thudding of fear almost at once – felt the white light – which this time fell in an oblong patch at the far side of the cave, a white oblong patch – like the timetable in the bus shelter, where her father had been, under the tiny print, the Bridport to Waytown bus schedule – where her father had been kissing and growling and thrusting with a woman whose face was lost under his –

Melanie saw Laurie and a man, locked together on the floor of the cave, under the oblong patch of light. Then the light went out. Melanie went up the path, to tell on Laurie, to join Bess. But, as so often happened with Melanie in her clumsy troublemaking, her playground tell-tale-tit, it was too late.

Twenty-five

MUFFLED DRUMS. VILLAGES along the coast of southern Dorset have heard them, or have given reports they have heard them, since the late sixteenth century, the time when stone birds flew at midnight from the gatepost of the manor house to the lake to drink, and black fairies appeared to innocent old women, and the sound of the sea fell at the sound of the drums coming over the water. It won't be the first time, either, that the drums tell of a death – of someone who disappeared and was heard again only in the thump of the drums, on nights when the sea is unexpectedly still. In an Indian summer, or in the halcyon days that come sometimes at midwinter, the drums beat as loud as a band, with a screeching of gulls as pipers overhead. On this calm October day, when the fog cleared and the drums came muffled in with its last whiteness on the coastal hills, a search party set out to find a group of missing girls. They could swear, later, that they had heard the sound of drums – but they didn't any of them like to say so at the time. For fear of sounding superstitious, no doubt; or seeming mad;

but the drums were real enough, in the dark, quiet night over the sea.

Jane walks ahead. She holds the axe, a long stone tied with a handkerchief to a stick – and she carries another handkerchief, for the blindfold. Behind her, Mary, who has come out on the side of the English Queen – her twin is down in the cave, with Melanie and the French Queen – Melanie the traitor, who had to go back to the cave because Bess ordered her out of the way, and Mathilda, the sister who has now turned in hatred against her twin. After Mary, Nat, who walks in a dream, head up to the bright half-moon and eyes half-closed – and after Nat, Bess's loyal troops, who were given the hair test in the cave (an old Abbotsbury game, this, and it never fails: a strand of hair between finger and thumb, curly is treacherous, straight is steadfast: lucky they've all been shown to be straight). The loyal army bangs the drum – empty Smartie packets, one old oil canister which makes all the din, so people really can hear on the coast – and they march down the winding path, to the cave over the black stones, to the theatre of execution where a black rock, lit sinisterly by the moon, awaits its prey.

What happens next can be seen pictured in any child's history book. It has the same air of unreality – can people really have acted like that – chopped off heads and in public – can these small people, no bigger than children are now, have sincerely believed in witches, in the divine right of kings? The picture is minuscule and far away. Yet when we crane to look closer, and the picture comes into focus, we recognise in it something we once knew, know still. We see the white boulder rolled away, and a huddle of figures. We hear the terrible drums. Then a cloud passes over the moon. It's cold: after all, it is October: Class Four's teeth chatter, from cold and fear.

The act of execution, that we can't see. The drums die away, water laps over the black stones, someone slips and falls. We don't see Bess either, for she never came to witness the beheading of her rival. If we turn, and stumble up the path under the sky thick with black clouds, we may see her on her ledge, upright and staring out over the sea. Perhaps she can hear her courtiers there, dancing to the beat of the drums – and then she hears the silence, before the waves strike up again.

Postscript

On the morning of Tuesday October 20th a group of girls was found by a search party consisting of assorted parents, schoolteachers and social workers:

they were found in the lane on the way to Mapperton, for the search party had gone in the wrong direction once they reached the coast, heading for Lyme Regis rather than Weymouth, and had had to retrace their footsteps entirely. The girls were tired and dirty, but seemed otherwise unsurprised by their adventure – it was as if, as Ms Potts remarked, they had just come back from one of their ordinary walks. Bess and Jane were reunited with Mr and Mrs Plantain; the parents of Class Four ran about in the lane hugging and holding their children; shyly, Laurie allowed her mother Mrs Strang to take her by the hand and lead her, as if she were a much younger child, to the estate wagon which had brought the party from Forton Court. Nat smiled at her mother, but could give no information in reply to her questions. The twins, together again after the first and only disruption in their lives, were equally unwilling to give anything away. It had been sunny in the days and cold at night, yes: they had roasted and eaten a swan (here a gasp went up). They stood meekly beside their teacher father, in the tribunal by the Posy Tree. So, at first, it was decided that the girls were too drained by their exposure to remember anything – must be taken to their respective homes and fed and washed – must sleep the frightening time away before they were subjected to any more questioning.

It was only as the group went off down the lane, leaving the Posy Tree and heading for the part of the road that was wide enough for their cars, that Ms

Potts's voice could be heard over the sounds of general reunion: 'Where's Melanie?'

Ms Potts's voice came down over the hedgerows, reached Mr and Mrs Plantain who, with a daughter at each side of them, didn't even turn round to hear her.

'Where's Melanie?' For Melanie's parents hadn't come, of course . . . and no one had missed her before. It went unanswered, Ms Potts's plaintive voice – and so did the mystery of the disappearance of Melanie, whose body, headless if only the grown-ups knew it, was later recovered from the sea. 'Where's Melanie?' – at least Ms Potts had found a pair of spectacles, crushed, on the ground by the Posy Tree, and had identified them as Melanie's. But that hardly helped.

The twins dawdled by their father's battered Mini, discussing the affair in low voices.

'So she did wear glasses after all.' Mary has on her most smug, know-all expression. Mathilda assumes hers too, gives a grave, self-satisfied nod.

'Maybe that's how she let herself get caught. She couldn't see Jane coming.'

'Couldn't see who?' says the twins' father as he rounds the car and leans over them. He has plenty of experience of eavesdropping on children's conversations. But the twins have always been too smart for him.

'I just said the fog was so thick I couldn't see anyone,' said Mary.

The twins' father frowned, then shrugged, decided to forget all about it. He had seen perfectly well that his daughters had glanced up the road at the Plantain girls as they spoke – but who was to know which one they referred to? Bess, steady, sensible Bess, or Jane, who looked different in some way today, but it was hard to tell why. He disliked the Plantains and banged the door of his Mini with particular force, to show the contrast between their luxurious car and his old and ruined one. He liked Laurie, though, she tried hard at maths and history, and he was glad to see her safely home.

Addendum

Since collating the material presented here – and as we go to press with this assortment of suggestions in book form – various facts pertaining to the walk of October 17th have come to light. I shall set them down in a perfunctory manner. I include also a short bibliography of works of reference found to be of use in the process of reconstruction.

It would be in the worst possible taste for any element of self-congratulation to be displayed at the accuracy of the unravelling of the tragic events of that walk down to the Isle of Portland. But (and deepest sympathy is of course proffered to the parents) Melanie Ayres's body was in fact found three days later, washed up on Chesil Bank. And, appalling though it is to be forced to state this, the body was indeed headless. What I had surmised – that a ritual game between pubescent girls, never intended to result in an actual execution, but tragically taken over by a girl suffering the most extreme form of identity crisis (that girl being Jane Plantain) – would now be difficult to contest.

Melanie Ayres 'pushed Jane over the edge', as it were, with her tales of changelings at a time when Jane was desperate to find her real self and avoid the labelling she had suffered since infancy from her mother. In return, she was murdered and literally pushed into the sea herself. (As further corroboration of our theory, we have heard that Jane's stutter has completely vanished, her nervous uncertainty having disappeared since her positive and destructive act.)

One aspect of the whole matter that is particularly unsavoury is Melanie's role as victim – class victim, ugliness victim – with all the disadvantages which would cause a 'well brought-up' and (her mother's daughter) presumably snobbish girl from the counties (such as Jane) to dislike her intensely anyway.

Yet it must be said that no one liked Melanie, and for all her aggression she was the one most likely to suffer the consequences of mass schoolgirl hysteria on the walk where they all became too dramatically, unnecessarily, lost. Melanie would have encouraged this atmosphere of drama, one can only suppose, with her belief in nuclear magic emanating from the girl she longed to reciprocate her love.

Dr Ross of Taunton has now made it known that Bess has resumed treatment and has, equally, lost her cough and other nervous symptoms since the cathartic walk of October 17th. He adds that he suspects, however, the cause of Bess's well-being will come to light soon as being the consequence of the banning of 'Uncle' from Forton Court for ever. It was indeed true that Bess only reported 'Uncle's' behaviour with Mrs Strang to her father when 'Uncle' made a play to seduce Laurie – and Bess's jealousy was of Laurie, of course, which Dr Ross regrets not having explored and understood earlier. Now the source of the problems has gone, the girls will no doubt continue in their fantasy world of kings and queens until such time as they are ready to enter the adult world.

Laurie, who had been pushed away by her mother in jealousy at the growing girl's attraction for 'Uncle', has been readmitted to the maternal bosom which, as her journal showed, she so desperately craved.

The twins, Nat, and Class Four of St Jude's, appear to have recovered remarkably quickly from their ordeal – indeed, the young ones have already a very hazy memory of the duration of the trip. The twins can be observed to be slightly more competitive with each other than before, but this is, it seems, producing excellent results in the science laboratory at Ferndale.

Nat, who was suffering from 'psychogenic disturbance of vision' at the time of seeing her father in the sea – and this, according to her mother, was certainly not the first time – has shown marked improvement. She is less dreamy, her mother has come to understand she must be encouraged to be practical; and it does seem apparent that to an imaginative child of this type the actual witnessing of a disaster can have a curative effect.

Dr Ross's footnote to a recent letter concerning Bess I reproduce below. Dr Ross writes: 'It may be of use to your "reconstruction" of the events of the weekend of October 17th if I inform you that on the day after the return from the walk, Bess Plantain was first introduced to her menstrual cycle. I had been expecting this for some time, of course; but, as often happens with neurotic patients, it needed a violent shock to bring it about.'

Dr Ross's information cannot cause much surprise. At times of upheaval a psychic quality is very often present in a developing female, and I have no doubt that Bess went deliberately off down the path to the coast – when she had seen, in her mind, the red spots of the plague by the Posy Tree – when she could sense the coming of a bloody adventure, the killing of a child, and her own first spots, in the curse of women, the plague – as she began to bleed.

January 1, 1982

Short Bibliography

Bruno Bettelheim, *The Uses of Enchantment*, Thames and Hudson, London, 1976

Sándor Ferenczi, *Thalassa: A Study of Genitality*, Psycho-Analytic Quarterly Inc., New York, 1938

Sigmund Freud, *Case Histories, Vol. 1: Dora* and *Little Hans*, Penguin, London, 1977

Iona and Peter Opie, *The Lore and Language of Schoolchildren*, Clarendon Press, Oxford, 1959

Donald W. Winnicott, *The Piggle*, Hogarth Press, London, 1978

Stefan Zweig, *Mary, Queen of Scots*, Cassell and Co., London, 1935.

ALICE FELL

For Olwyn

MR PAXTON WENT down to the river. It was late on a spring evening. He went without looking back – at the house, where the Old Man held like a clam to the greater proportion of corridors and half-furnished rooms – at the bright window above the back-door that was frame to the midwife's busyings. He walked with purpose, and nervously. Tall irises, machete-shaped, fell under his feet.

At that hour, the Old Man saw his friends. Something in the acid blue of the air, the yellow irises like lights on the river, the smell of blossom, intoxicated the Old Man and made him think of his youth. His arms rose and fell, as if he were conducting. He bowed to his friends Molly and Pam and rushed them to the window, so they could see the stars stitched above vague apartment blocks, blocks of darker colour round the house as deep as the trunks of trees.

In the spring that Mr Paxton went down to the river, and the midwife made ready above the back-door, the Old Man showed no sign that anything new was happening in the house. He moved around in his part of it carelessly, like a troll in a great bed. He called for

Mrs Paxton, and showed no surprise when only her husband came.

On this night, while Anthony Eden pronounced on the Suez crisis and the Old Man spoke to Molly and Pam, and there was a bear market which would have no effect on Mr Paxton because he owned no shares, and rockets were being constructed that would one day go to the moon, Mr Paxton arrived at his destination of the river and the moon came up behind him. The moon also shone in the window where the midwife stood black against the light. Over the Old Man's part of the house the stars vanished in dust as he pointed them out to the visitors. A mist came up over the river. Now the Old Man wanted ice for the drinks, and he went to the kitchen, not knowing what he would find.

Mrs Grogan the midwife laughed when she was asked to produce ice. She was doing different things with water: drawing hot clouds from the kettle which turned to tears on the walls, pressing towels damped with the precious hot water, folding newspapers that took a sudden boldness at the water's touch. She was about to carry the whole lot up the stairs behind the kitchen. Mrs Paxton lay in the room there, between the shadow of the ash tree on the wall, and the window, and the moon. Mrs Grogan flung open the kitchen door before leaving.

'Go and get it for yourself,' she said.

Mrs Grogan had no need to show politeness to the Old Man. She was here as a favour for Mrs Paxton. She had known Mr and Mrs Paxton in the old days, when Mr Paxton had been in the chemist's in the small town, before he got nervous and came to work for the Old Man. Mrs Grogan had watched Mr Paxton pouring red and yellow streams into bottles, and then when it was all tablets and capsules she had talked to Mr Paxton as he slid them into perspex containers. She had no respect at all for the Old Man. He lingered in the house of his birth when long ago he should have been out in the world, or been at sea or war. If the Old Man came to the kitchen, in his folly assuming there would be eggs in a brown basket on the table, and that by some process they would leap to the pan and make a supper for him, she snorted in contempt.

In the room where Mrs Paxton waited for Mrs Grogan, the lamp had been turned off. Agony belonged to night and would take advantage of the union, increase the whirligig of pain. In the dark, from where Mrs Paxton could see, the room was nevertheless invaded in three ways by light. The moon floated in the open upper window and too close. Mrs Paxton saw it on a steel tripod, examining with a critical eye the humps of her mountain body;

then the moon on the ash tree made a white, ghostly rectangle on the wall opposite the bed; and once again the moon, reflected in the Old Man's bedroom window opposite, came in on the rebound and cut her down the middle carelessly, as she lay waiting for the hot water and towels.

Mrs Grogan climbed the stairs. As the Old Man went on with his conversation, his arabesque with the past, the house turned in darkness to the tops of the trees and the downs. The tops of the trees and the downs moved towards the house in the darkness. They rose above Mr Paxton as he walked to the river. The moon, too, passed over Mr Paxton. The downs above the house and the water-meadows to the south of the river, as they pulled the house and trees with them into night, had as little sense of the impending birth of the Paxtons' child as the Old Man. Only Mr Paxton knew something was going to happen. But he couldn't see exactly what.

The Old Man took the ice and went to sit with Molly and Pam in the room furthest away from the stables, and the Paxtons' part of the house. In wresting the ice from its tray, his fingers had wrinkled and the nails were water frozen to bone. A tapestry woven with blue wools, and showing the pained eyes and long tresses of the women loved by the Symbolists, hung on the wall behind him.

Mrs Grogan arrived in Mrs Paxton's room. The three lines of light came out to her, and, swaying with her kettle, she nearly lost her step and fell into the web. She went with care to Mrs Paxton. She wanted to draw the child, smocked in white cream from the womb, into the world. Mrs Grogan turned on the light and knelt down by the bed. When she looked up she saw only the moon, and the ash tree upright outside the window, in a silver forceps over the bed.

Now the light was on in Mrs Paxton's room, a bowl went down and water from the kettle was poured in.

'Up she comes' and 'Push!' Mrs Grogan was saying. 'What a farmyard! Move the farmyard, Mrs Paxton!'

Mrs Paxton saw a fairy feast, tightly enclosed behind her red, throbbing eyes. There was dancing, and every so often a shower of red balloons sprang out over the dancers and exploded in the air. In the clasp of her body, she felt feet tramp through halls where the roof was pulled down and down. Soon the roof would come right down on the tables, and crush the metal spoons, and then she would be shot out, like a woman from a cannon, into the void. Her body heaved and shuddered. It was a fight to the death between the woman and the child.

Mrs Grogan had bowls of water all round the bed. She sponged the new mother's face, which looked garish and unreal, a painted face of the dead at the entrance to the tomb. She laid newspapers under the vaults of Mrs Paxton. Despite the drama, Mrs Grogan thought of her own daughter who was coming over from the other side of the world, and how that girl should never have married Bob and fallen down there, and how she would be in time for the daffodils. It was unlikely to Mrs Grogan that there were such things as daffodils on the other side of the world. Only white flowers could grow there, very probably, as it was so dark.

Mrs Paxton groaned, and water came from her. Newspapers were flooded and Mrs Grogan rushed to change them: Suez Crisis and *Woman's Own* and in a last rush an old *Picture Post*. Winston Churchill was pushed under Mrs Paxton's monumental legs and lay in the water. His face frowned, and dissolved. 'Push down!' shouted Mrs Grogan.

M R PAXTON ARRIVED at the edge of the river. The moon had completely deserted him and without light his hearing had grown foggy so he didn't hear the moans from his wife as her waters broke. He stared out anxiously instead across the river. He might have been expecting a visitor from the other shore. Mr Paxton tried to see the opposite bank, but mist obscured his view. He lit a match once, and saw his feet helpless in mud. In his sudden aura he stood in a dome of glass. Mr Paxton felt his absolute lack of necessity. He stood still in his crumpled suit until the match went out. The mist had taken perspective from his sight, but he was still waiting for something. Reeds flanked him, like an army of porcupines. The black river flowed invisibly under his feet.

Mist rose in furrows in the ground. In the cold spring night the earth breathed white steam, from the great flat mouth of the earth that was buried under grass and poplars. Mist took away the borders of the river and changed it to sea.

Mr Paxton looked out in expectation. He was the last man of the old world. He saw sails of a ship in the mist. Then he thought he saw the swan that lived in the bend in the river, coming towards him over the sea with mist-furled wings. He was the last man who could read the writing of the old world. Mud under his feet changed to sand, and the reeds, dipped in the ink-black sea, wrote for him on the white sand. The floating strands of mist took the messages out over the water again, and still Mr Paxton peered, hand over his eyes, a man lost at sea in a mist.

What was in the chest?

The chest lay at Mr Paxton's feet. It had come out of the sea. Mr Paxton thought of all the diseases that might be in it, or sea-serpents that would wriggle over his feet.

Mr Paxton opened the chest. It was small, bound with rope, and dry inside. He lifted out the infant. There was a letter pinned to the infant's dress. Mr Paxton could read the writing. The note said the infant had been abandoned. Mr Paxton couldn't read the signature. He set off for the house, holding the infant. As he got near to the house he heard Mrs Grogan's voice, leaping from Mrs Paxton's window to the ash tree and hanging in a string of vowels in the line between the ash tree and the moon.

That was how it was known the child had been born. Mr Paxton had a piece of paper, which told him he had custody of this daughter. She was not his, how could she be his, and although there was no paper to

168

inform him of the day he would have to part with her, he saw the day quite clearly, as he stood in Mrs Paxton's room, and he even saw the man who would come to claim her.

Mrs Paxton was alone and free, beside the burst bubble of water where her daughter had lived. She was bled out, and Mrs Grogan had cut the cord and tied the remains of it in the shape of a piglet's tail. Mrs Paxton lay on her side, as if expecting the infant to climb up to a row of nipples. Mrs Grogan, packing a bag, said she would accept a lift from Mr Paxton and would collect the bicycle tomorrow. Mr Paxton went after her, walking on the tips of his toes. Mrs Paxton was supposed to be sleeping, and so was the infant, in its chest in the corner.

The Old Man's house grew silent with the going of Mr Paxton and Mrs Grogan, and it absorbed the existence of the child. There was silence, and the Old Man went to bed in absolute silence, as if taking the punishment for his earlier flippancy. For all the millions already in the world, something had happened. Mrs Paxton lay still, as if it were she who had had her lifeline severed. And the moon turned a fuller face down on her, spoon-feeding Mrs Paxton as she lay breathing softly on the bed.

The Old Man, despite his efforts to sit in distant rooms or to forget the coming of the child altogether, was caught by it in the end. For the moon, in going into Mrs Paxton's room, and down into the fork of the ash tree, was reflected that night in the Old Man's bedroom window. Before he could wake properly and stop it, he saw the film the moon played: in light conducted from the ash tree, the spool of the birth was played relentlessly, before the Old Man's windows and his half-closed eyes.

WHEN DAY CAME, it seemed at first that the breathing of the child was no different from the wind in the trees, the stirring of bushes by the river at the wind's plunge. The cries of the child were a distant cutting: trees fell, giving out flakes of red dust as the chain of high sound bit the bark. The Old Man walked down to the river, and up the path to the swan's nest. Two jagged lily cups of shell floated on the water. It was possible to see a dash of brown fur in the nest, as if a mole, burrowing in the earth, had come suddenly up in a straw hat. But the Old Man told Mr Paxton he had seen two cygnets there. He wondered that they should have come out of one egg. He suggested there might have been another egg, hidden. That was as far as he would go, in accepting a new child living and breathing in his house.

Mrs Grogan had returned to her house in the small town. Spring, always later than expected, moved down a few inches in the trees and then jammed again. A pallor hung over the downs and the house and spread itself – to the campions, still wink-shut, to the cows swishing their tails in the still, white air, to the people in the country town, moving between the baker's, and the butcher's, and the chemist's where Mr Paxton used to work. When the sun came out, it hung in a white ball in the sky. Then the sharp wind from the east would unravel it, and it skittered into clouds.

In the room above the kitchen it seemed that the child and her mother had been permanently bedded down. The child's eyes seldom opened, and when they did there was only a muddy blue, like sky reflected in a puddle. The child's fingers waved constantly. But they could grasp nothing. They couldn't even move in time with Mrs Paxton's clock, which measured a day completely at odds with the child's. At the end of the cot, a white woollen ball was suspended on a string. In the faint draught from the door, the ball swayed in a pendulum, and the child followed its course through the heavens. The child's eyes flickered from side to side at the swaying of the white sun which rose in the east at the last bar of the cot, and set behind Mrs Paxton.

Mrs Grogan had other things to think about than the child she had delivered with her own hands from Mrs Paxton. Her daughter Ella had arrived, and would not be going back to Bob. Mrs Grogan was overjoyed. 'I always told you,' she said, 'I told you, why do' you have to go all that way to be with someone and it's not even a proper job. Why should he drag you down there. It's a long way to go to the other side of the world and there's no house waiting. Come live with me, he says, but where. Well, you're here now.'

Mrs Grogan's daughter Ella was not happy, however. She had to go to the chemist's, where Mr Paxton sometimes sneaked back for the afternoon as he missed making up prescriptions, and ask for tablets. 'You'll have to have a job,' Mrs Grogan said. 'So I said to Mrs Paxton, as Mrs Paxton has to cook and clean for the Old Man, why doesn't Ella look after the baby?'

Ella first saw the child when her eyes were full of tears and the child was crying too, so they saw each other blurred, with the ash tree leaning in at them from the window. Mrs Paxton was no more than a smudge against the pillows. Ella told the child how she had floated, dizzy, by the church at the boundary of the garden, and in her red dream measured by Mr Paxton, Ella had thought of fighting her way under the stone or running, in short zig-zags, to the river and jumping in. Instead she had somehow found herself with the child. Ella and the child gazed at the soft ball of white wool that swung at the end of the cot and Ella put her head to one side, as if considering this new, shrunken world she had come to live in. She wondered, too, whether she would ever get out the other side and find a world that fitted round her, or whether, as she had known when she went down into Australia and married Bob, it always fell open at the back.

O N THOSE SPRING nights when the child had just been born and Britain held on to its old possessions with no intention of letting them go, the Old Man visited the far side of the house for days at a time, in an attempt to live life as it once had been. His father and elder brothers waited for him in the smoking-room, where smoke from their cigars rose to maps on the walls and made peace over deserts, whitening the Russian steppes newly gone to the Reds. The Old Man stepped carefully between these velvet-jacketed men of Empire, who sat on buttoned thrones with stubby feet. He went through side-doors that opened with a sharp smell of dust, and led him to rooms where there were only watering-cans and windows that were too high to look out at the downs. He had a sense of the ending of things, and the beginning of something he would never understand. He looked at the green watering-cans, and thought of his grandmother laying flowers in a basket. The women who had heated her water and brushed her hair had lived here. They had carried coal to the big furnace, to heat the water to wash her hair. His grandmother had placed the flowers in a white vase the shape of a hand.

In his desire to find comfort, the Old Man visited the men who sat forever at a green baize table – despite the changing seasons, despite the years which bit at the legs of the table and made round holes – they sat forever at a green baize table playing cards. Or the Old Man went to the furthest side of the house from the Paxtons. He crossed landings, and went through rooms that were there for the sole purpose of going through at times like these: rooms that looked out only on his land and could comfort him in his solipsistic view; rooms with windows that held the hills securely rounded in their frames, an amphitheatre to the Old Man's sighs. And the rooms were closely connected, in a cousinage of Persian carpet and black portraits gone green. There were none of the distances in the far side of the house that kept him always at arm's length from the Paxtons in their rooms, or flattened him in corners when he saw them coming. Here, the faces of dead aunts and uncles winked through open doors, and merged together sometimes into one mournful, quizzical face. The Old Man thought he would very soon join them, as a pore on a sallow cheek or a black hair in an eyebrow that refuses to lie down. Following the line of those self-important, undistinguished men and women, the Old Man could come to the room at the furthest side of the house, where the Blue Women hung on the wall between the windows and so had to look into the room, and away from the freedom of the hills: there they could concentrate on him alone.

The Blue Women had been such a time without freedom that their faces and limbs, once sewn in supple lines, had grown stiff and brittle. A group of young women they had been once, with one of the Old Man's great-aunts at the centre of the group, who had sung at the piano downstairs and been worshipped from afar, and even then the small freedom of their age taken from them and the tapestry closing round, the exact place allotted mercilessly in the *petit point*, with live children and dying children in bright colours, and perhaps in the foreground a happy little animal. There was no way of knowing, when the Old Man went to the furthest room, whether the Blue Women could feel the shock of a birth of a child in the house. One of the women at the back, who was pulling at a branch, pulling it down to her like a finger in a knitted glove, appeared to be pregnant. She was in a Florentine gown, and as she stood there, the woollen twig forever embedded in her bosom, she seemed in those first days of the life of the child to look out with anguish at the Old Man and the confining room. She could hear the child's cries at night, even at this distance – and the Old Man looked at her in concern, for he wanted nothing to disturb the silence and calm of the Blue Women. To the Old Man, the chatter of Molly and Pam, members of the generation of women that had succeeded the Blue Women, was intolerable at this time, although he often in his loneliness invited them. These women of the twenties and thirties, cropped and flat as they sprang from the shears, never looking back at their mothers lying there behind them, grated on his nerves like the tang of lemon peel they put in their cocktails or the bright beads of saliva that came to the corners of their painted mouths as they talked. The Old Man liked only the peace of the furthest room, where the Blue Women had long ago destroyed any words that might have described them. He hoped no intrusion from the Paxtons could ever come there, although in fact it was already too late for him to express this hope.

The child, whom the Paxtons had named Alice, slept only a few hours in the night, so that she woke every hour to new days, and dreamed through them, and then plunged into night again, making a calendar with whole months that would never be recalled, and anniversaries between each suck at the breast.

And as she lay dreaming and waking, and the Old Man wandered about in his insomnia in the house, the white sun at the end of her crib fell and rolled away into the corridors in the dark. Mrs Paxton didn't notice, as she nodded and dozed over the local paper Mr Paxton had brought with tea. The soft ball of white wool rolled soundlessly. It left the Paxtons in their rooms, and it rolled to the far side of the Old Man's house.

THE BALL WENT to the blue tapestry in the room where the Old Man liked to sit. It hung from a tree in the glade where the women reclined and brushed their hair. They looked up at it with their bright, blue woollen eyes. It hung innocently above them, in the shape of an apple. But they knew already that it brought trouble – from the other side of the house, from the new womanhood that had burst out there – and the women stirred, uneasy in the embroidered glade. They had been there too long, and had fulfilled too many expectations: of languor, repressed desire, and maternal devotion; and they reached out their hands to the woven fruit, as if they wished it would fall to them, and reveal a new knowledge. But when it did fall, they only threw it back up in the air again. The Blue Women had little real wish to know the new world being born outside the Old Man's house.

A T THIS TIME, when England was trying to hold on, to keep what remained to it of the imperial dignity of the past, the first beat of a new sound came over the downs and the Old Man stood aghast at the window. He heard wailing, and a totemic beat, as the first sound of men brought up not to fight came in its loud lamentation from the woods, and the Old Stones danced to the radio. And he turned to speak to Mrs Grogan, who had come into the room to clean: he spoke of the collapse of belief in civilisation between the wars, and the wreck of all the sacred spaces, from industrialisation and this search for equality, and the people everywhere, in caravans and each moment losing the desire to fight for king and country. Now he wanted to know where this din came from. But Mrs Grogan wasn't sure. She didn't like the new race of young men, in black leather jackets and badgers' faces. She disliked the way they hung around Ella, and said they'd take her off to the pier at Brighton, where they would stomp, and menace, and hold her up against the palisade.

The Old Man watched Mrs Grogan intently as she continued her dusting of the room with the blue tapestry. He felt the spring relayed to him in an unacceptable manner. He wanted slow buds unfolding and a harmless appearance of green leaf, a ragged bunting in the trees, fairy lights set up crooked in the chestnuts. He was sent instead this raw pulse of young men stretching and shooting into idleness.

Mr Paxton was an anxious father in the spring of the birth of the child. He thought the child needed the ball at the end of the crib, and that without it, the endless minutes in her days would go unremarked, pile up, until after an avalanche of unrecorded time she would emerge suddenly old. He had no way of trusting Mrs Paxton's knowledge of time, which was measured off with knitting needles and the thud of the arrival on the kitchen table of a cup of tea. He said, if the ball could be got back, everything would be at normal again, like before.

Ella, as she went about repairing an old pram found in one of the disused lower rooms, was hardly inclined to agree with this. She had long ago set her clock to be with Bob at the other side of the world, and his minutes marched against hers. There, leaves were falling and settling into the earth. She had no interest in the pushing up of shoots, because even the deepest of them could in no way come out the other side and

179

tie a tendril about the neck of her Bob. Buds were the same: Ella looked at them as if they were warheads. She pushed the pram with the child lying folded inside shawls, over the wrong side of the earth. In the thicket down by the river she searched for a hole in the mulch of old leaves. There had been an air-raid shelter in that spot once, Mr Paxton said. It was deep, so if the Germans had come they would have seen nothing and flown away again. Ella was rash in wanting to jump into that roofless house, with walls of leaves, as if she hoped to dive into a cellar where Bob lay waiting. She was bound to upset the child one day. Mr Paxton swore he would keep a strict eye on Ella, and that he would find the ball.

WITH THE RELUCTANCE and artificiality of the spring Molly and Pam came more and more often; and this the Old Man hated, for now he wanted to be alone. The plastics that had sprouted after the war in his new quarters at the top of the house where the Paxtons placed units with imitation wood handles and linos in triangles of black and white made the Old Man gaze at his surroundings in misery. There was nothing he could feel for here. He listened with a dull expression while Molly and Pam prattled of the new luxuries that had come at last to this country where they had been obliged for so long to wear grey flannel and eat inferior food. He listened gravely, with his arms around his knees, to the talk of rhinestones, and planes that worked by jet, and dresses that were 'strapless', held up by a whale under the dress that propelled these new dancers over an ocean of parquet, under marquees of the most exquisite nylon net. The Old Man nodded, hearing of the return of extravagance and waste. 'But you must come up to London with us,' Molly said. 'These are an example,' said Pam, as she took off an ear-ring. 'Wouldn't you think they were real?'

In the shower of over-bright stones that Pam was waving, one broke free and flew out of the window that gave on the garden. But there was a whole spray of stones there, and it went unmissed: 'People put their real jewellery in the bank nowadays,' said Pam, 'and wear rhinestones like this. Don't you think it's wonderful?'

The child may have seen the glass ball as it went over her. The sun had come out, and Mr Paxton was pushing her in the pram, over grass and white daffodils and primroses. The blue in the sky filled the glass ball, and the child may have looked up and caught its eye, as muddled and blue as hers. But Mr Paxton saw only his child's missing ball: as he raised his head in time to see the sun vanish behind clouds and the clouds come down to enfold the ball, he turned sharply and went after it, as it bounced now in the long grass on the way down to the river.

Pam put her ear-ring back in, as Ella ran to the reeds and the boggy land down by the river. She knew where the ball might have led Mr Paxton and his child. Mrs Paxton looked out in surprise, from the kitchen, as she rolled pastry and scrumpled it up again.

Mr Paxton had put flowers in the pram. Ella saw the flowers, the white flowers of that spring, on the water near the swan's nest. The child and her father were nowhere to be seen. The pram was overturned and empty, like an old piece of scrap-metal on that river-bank. Behind her, the Old Man strolled with Molly and Pam, out to take some air of the cold, late spring. The Old Man nodded in pleasure, at seeing the trans-mutation of the ball, the ball which had led Mr Paxton into danger and therefore the infant too, perhaps killing it, so he would no longer have to put up with its unacceptable, unnameable existence. The Old Man imagined the infant under the water, where it had sunk in the ooze, dropped by its father as he tried to swim over to retrieve the ball. He hoped Mr Paxton would rise soon, shaking himself and cold with the black water, on the far bank, and would care for him as he had in earlier days, bringing magazines and a silver pot of coffee out to a hammock under lilac in the garden. So the Old Man looked intently at the egg in the swan's nest in the middle of the river. He looked at the white ball of shell that had hung at Molly's ear as a false diamond, and had measured the days at the end of the infant's cot in an orb of white wool. And he pointed it out to Molly and Pam, but they looked away in scorn. A swan's egg had no place in their new world – of square blocks going up in the mess left by the war, and chemicals that grew into diamonds without even having to enter the crust of the earth.

Mr Paxton's cries could be heard from the wood. Molly and Pam went fussily after the Old Man, and with their heels speared dockets of dead leaves. They wanted the sun, which would turn the white flowers gold, and not the clumps of bamboo rising to damp beech and alder. By the lair in which the Old Man and Mr Paxton would have crouched if the bombers had come over, they paused and looked in through gloom the colour of leaf rotted to web. They heard the child wailing in there. And Mr Paxton thrashing about uselessly in the part that was to have been the larder, with cans of soup and an opener in case Mrs Paxton got bombed on the way from the house with a hot meal on a tray. Neither Molly nor Pam nor the Old Man had the slightest desire to scramble in the leaves, pulling the victims out.

After Ella had gone down, unblocked the entrance to the larder, and Mr Paxton had come out holding the child, and had had to look Ella in the eye and thank her for rescuing him from her own stupid accident, Mr Paxton was never so certain again of his rightness in handling matters concerning his family. He left the ball alone, and gave no advice to Mrs Paxton. But the fall provided the Old Man with some amusement. For, as the child was lifted from the hole, and the dying white flowers clenched in her fist turned yellow in the sun that poked down through the trees for the first time, the Old Man named her, and accepted the reality of her being in the world. He turned first to Molly and Pam – but they had gone, the sudden coming of the spring was too real for them – and he said: to himself, to the woods: 'Persephone!'

When Alice fell, and the Old Man walked back to the house alone, he went at a slow pace and with stooped shoulders. He was suddenly old since acknowledging the existence of the child and witnessing her first fall; made thoughtful by the great confusion of things around him all happening at the same time: the cater-wauling on the downs that was birth-shriek to the new age, the end of him and the end of the line ushered in by a child that was female and, despite the changes he could see coming so clearly, unlikely to have any choice other than that of falling. The Old Man went to the furthest room, and looked at the Blue Women and then out of the window at the downs. The sudden arrival of Alice in this house filled him with unease and misgivings. He no longer knew if the women in the tapestry, his tormented idols, had also fallen, from lack of fulfilment, lack of love or ambitions realised, into their attitudes of woven despair. He saw, for a moment as the clouds danced like buffoons before being blown away altogether to the valleys beyond the downs, that Molly and Pam had fallen too in their effort to be independent, to be new. Their faces were hollow with children refused. Under the bright shingle, their mothers' minds raced, and tossed them against the cliffs of insecurity, domestic catastrophe, divorce. And on their slim legs, as they danced, and fell, and drank and smoked, the tides of the years' fashions went up and down, in hemlines that had more meaning than their lives.

In her sleep, as the child fell and spring came down suddenly from the trees to scoop the child, to fill the scoop where it had fallen with violets and crocuses, and to rock the child, safe now in its pram, in winds from south and west, a cat's cradle of winds that lifted ribbons from the bonnet of the child and wove them in invisible patterns in the air – in her sleep, into which she had plunged as surely as her daughter had fallen down the hole, Mrs Paxton dreamed. She was bound to a post, out at sea. She cried, against the birds, and the terrible noise of the sea, which ran past her with always somewhere further to go. The cold sea, cold as the spring, might take heat on the surface, from the sun, but underneath it was all black hair, greasy and cold and black, under the tinted strand. Mrs Paxton cried to be heard. But the men and women on the shore could no more hear her than they could the birds, nor could they hear the ponderous message the waves laid down on the stones, before going out again. Mrs Paxton was her own daughter, strapped and tied, and crying in a language not even her mother could understand. She was powerless, swaddled by the iron bands of the sea.

Mrs Paxton woke, to the burnt–out kettle and the shamed face of Ella, on the scene of damage as usual, but too late. 'Now what'll we do?' said Mrs Paxton, but in spite of her anger she could only remember the sea – and Ella's thick legs, which were like posts sticking up out of the sea, as she mopped water from the exploded kettle on the floor. 'See if you can't nip into Booth's and get us one,' Mrs Paxton added. 'If only we could have an electric kettle, what a difference that would make!'

Alice was brought into the house, with dread on the part of Mr Paxton. And Ella screamed, at the accident following her own desire to jump (unless they were all destined to fall to the other side of the world); and Mr Paxton frowned, and went to put on a pan of water. He had been custodian, of this child who had come to him washed up from nowhere, with a message that he must care for her. Instead of which, he had fallen with her on to leaves that had been brushed aside to reveal stubby crocus shoots, pointing up like missiles and bruised purple at the top. Now, of all things, there was no kettle. Mr Paxton put the pan on gingerly, as if the world had been declared at an end and they were all adapting to the savage life, with a muddy child on the floor at their feet.

Mrs Paxton went over every inch of the child when Ella had finished with it, then, sighing in relief once she knew there was no harm done, said – and again and again – 'Aren't you a clever little girl?' And: 'Wasn't she a clever girl, to find her way home then?'

Water boiled. Mr Paxton went over to the wireless in the corner and twiddled a knob, to hear news from Sir Anthony Eden. He would be reassured, to hear voices of men who spoke in a language neither his wife nor Ella nor the child on the floor could understand. He thought sternly of the loss of power in Suez. And he remembered, for Mr Paxton knew his nervousness when he saw Ella standing there, with the sun coming in under the door behind her in yellow stalks, and Ella seeing only her daffodils, and the face of Bob, that he had nearly lost his daughter and that he must once again return everything to normal as quickly as possible. He suggested a treat. 'After tea,' Ella was told, 'we'll go and visit the menagerie.'

THE OLD MAN'S menagerie lived in parts of the garden; but sometimes, when the time of the year was blank before spring, or the leaves fell too heavily, burying animals and reptiles and birds, fitting them out in newly stitched coats from which their eyes gleamed like diamond pins, they moved indoors and could be found in the five rooms of the house, that led off the main landing. Then, Mr Paxton went into the garden in vain. He stood in the emptiness of the stone-walled garden, where the old parrot had been, and on the grass by the river, stripped of colour now the green lizards had gone to the house to multiply, to make scaly green mountains in the room at the far end of the corridor, with so many blue eyes there was a sky flickering behind them. Mr Paxton shook his head in a mixture of rage and tolerance. He knew the presence in the house of these moving possessions of the Old Man's annoyed and upset Mrs Paxton. But he was glad to walk alone in the garden, especially with his daughter, rather than risk the sun covered by the wings of the parrot, and the lizards talking to the stones, with the child listening intently. He wanted to

provide the child with his own face, and her mother's
– but, unknown to him, it was already too late, for
the menagerie had sought out this new addition to
their ranks and for the few months she was theirs,
completely owned her: Mr Paxton's face, looming
above the child on afternoon walks, folded into wings
of purple and red, and as Mrs Paxton and Ella spoke
in the kitchen, green snakes fell from their mouths. If
the Old Man's butterflies hatched in the rooms, the
child was wrapped in their spotted skirts until she was
lifted, and put to the breast.

At this time of year, when spring was reluctant to
come and the Old Man had to stay in his rooms,
among the hills and glittering plains made by the
lizards – the old parrot high on a cupboard, like a
bunch of red blossoms in the unnatural spring – he
would sit over his boxes of photographs and pull out
the people he hoped to project on the walls of his
shadowy rooms. He saw his father's father, summoned in his photograph from the eternal room upstairs and standing with an expression of impatience
in the low hills of his land in the north. His beard was
white, and after him, in the sliding palms of the Old
Man's hands came the white beard of Freud, and then
there was a group of aunts of Molly and Pam, with
buttercup hats and pinched waists that looked ready
to be threaded with a needle and joined together for
life. The Old Man sighed, and remembered those
hats, with ribbons that stuck out behind in the wind,

then the aunts when they had become ill, and the hats forever on pegs in the hall. What had been wrong with these aunts would never be known, but the frames they had been placed in finally exploded, and they stopped dancing and fell into a swoon.

Sometimes, in the long days before the Old Man moved to the garden and took the menagerie with him, the photographs filled the house entirely. In the film of shadows in corners, and the sudden expanses of white on a wall, where a sitter had chosen a studio portrait, or where a white sky, firm as wax, was cut out around head and shoulders, there appeared the extreme anonymity of the Old Man's family, long-dead; and then the immortals, who rose from a scrap-book he had kept as a child, and transformed the house, just as they had formed the new age into which they had been born. Freud, and Alexander Fleming, and Rutherford – and Lenin and Jung and Joyce and Proust – and Stravinsky and Picasso and Yeats – walked in the house, and the shadows from the ash tree outside came in in the first rays of sun of the new spring and made libraries and laboratories, and orchestras in the creaking of the old house and the tossing of leaves on the ash tree outside, as they grew and unfurled in the sun. The immortals ignored the Old Man's family completely, as they walked in rooms that expanded or shrank as they entered, to suit their purpose. They looked at the aunts, and at Molly and Pam, and at the Blue Women, who had

wandered by mistake into this black and white photo-
graphic world, as if they were no more than specks of
dust, case-histories long pushed away in the archives,
specimens on slides, millions on millions of them, in a
discarded science of the past. They picked their way
with expressions of scorn through the Old Man's
rooms, and made for the kitchen wing. And they
lingered there, after everyone had gone to bed,
bringing black shadows, and a sudden exposure of
white, as the moon came in at the doors and lit up a
famous ear, or made a white turnip of a nose, or
removed altogether the top of a distinguished hat.
These great men had come to see Mrs Paxton, and
Ella, and the child. They came in threes, these Wise
Men, and stood loftily in the bright green room
where Mrs Paxton liked to have her last cup of tea
before feeding the child. They stared in great perplexity into the crib. When the Old Man threw down
the scrap-book, they vanished again. They might
never have been heard of by the Paxtons, and certainly there was no mention of them in the paper Mr
Paxton brought his wife, on his way back from a
quick evening pint. They might have been a figment
of the Old Man's imagination – but the house was
nervous with them when they walked in it – and it
seemed they had a fear that the child would destroy
the world they had made around them.

The Old Man was certainly not pleased to find his
ancestors despised in this way by the Immortals. He

arranged again and again the flowers in great blue and white urns, rugs were thrown over banisters and draped from ceilings as if he were trying to show his house as a tent, to prove to these condescending men the transitoriness of things; he went more and more frequently to the upper room, where his statesmen forebears conferred on the problem of the Suez crisis and sent orders, from behind the green baize door, into the outside world. Perhaps, as apprehensive as the Great Men and, unlike them unable to divine the probable cause of unrest to come, he was simply more sensitive than usual on the subject of his surroundings, of the world which enclosed him. He knew, too, that the world the child would inherit would be empty both of the Great Men and of him.

As all this went on, and the days became slowly longer, Mrs Paxton took to carrying Alice about the house and then back to the kitchen again. 'Where've you been?' Mr Paxton said; for he had a dread of Mrs Paxton meeting Freud or some such on those landings which were so uncertain at this time of year, with the odd light and the shadows. 'If I can't clean without leaving her strapped down somewhere, I'd like to know what I can do,' said Mrs Paxton. And at this point, always, Ella would come in and say: 'I dreamt of Bob again last night!' and 'What do you think it can mean?'

Mr Paxton invariably stood by the stove when these exchanges took place. Ella's coming from Australia, and the long cord of dreams that held her to Bob at the other side of the world, made him fear for his own daughter, and her place on the spinning ball, where she might lose her footing and slip into space. In the years before Alice was born, he wished only for his solitary talks with the parrot, and a chat with the chemist in the afternoon, and a listening to the news in the evening with his eyes trained on the face of Mrs Paxton, as if the information were issuing from her lips; but in the year the child was born he knew the wrong child had come to him and that he must remedy this.

'Lalla . . . Lalla . . . Lalla . . . ' sang Mrs Paxton at the cot.

'Lalla,' the child seemed to say, from a mouth festooned with spit.

'She said Ella,' Ella said.

'Lalla . . . Lalla . . . ' went on Mrs Paxton. 'Do you know, we haven't even got a rattle for her yet and that's because Mrs Grogan said the rattles at Sturgis were unhygienic and the Morton child had thrush from one. Don't you think it's a shame?'

Mr Paxton still kept very close to the stove, as if the kettle might jump at him if he didn't guard it. 'Nothing is unhygienic at Sturgis,' he said finally, for that was the chemist's where he had worked, and where he went still, to savour the pleasure of not being there at all hours, nervous in a white coat behind the little window that said Prescriptions.

'I'll make her a rattle, though. I'll make her one.'

'Make her one,' said Mrs Paxton. 'That's a funny idea.'

'I dreamt of Bob standing with his back to a bank of daffodils,' Ella said. 'Don't you think that must mean he's coming soon?'

Mr Paxton went from stove to old wireless, cautiously. Sometimes, in mid-movement, he was caught and hurled off on some errand, or told sharply there were the chairs to mend in the junk room over the stable. This time he was lucky. As the child gurgled, and Mrs Paxton improvised this lullaby as she scraped carrots for the Old Man's supper, he heard the news and nodded his head to the time of the announcer's Oxford tones. As the new ball of white wool, bought at the chemist by Mrs Grogan and tied firmly to the end of the cot, swung to and fro, and the child's eyes followed it and then trembled shut, the father heard the tramp of marchers in the room.

The marchers were marching against the bomb, as they went from Aldermaston into Trafalgar Square, and the tramping of boots made him think of the war. To the side of Mr Paxton his wife hummed and grated, like a song whistled through a comb. The

kitchen was dark, on the evening Mr Paxton understood that he would never be able to control or understand the events in the Old Man's house or in the
world beyond. For, as the boots marched in his radio
against a new ball of destruction he could never have
dreamed as a boy, and Mrs Paxton hummed in a
language only the child could hear, the white woollen
ball flew off again – unnoticed by any of them. Later,
when Mr Paxton questioned Ella and Mrs Paxton, he
did so without any of the certainty of retrieval he had
shown on earlier occasions. Like the Old Man, he
found the spectre of the bomb and the presence of
the child too unnerving. All Ella said was she could
have sworn, when Mr Paxton asked her later, that she
had seen a dumpling fly through the air, in the
cauldron of steam that was the kitchen, with Mrs
Paxton standing over the boiling water and only
portions of Mr Paxton and Ella visible in the mist.

At about this time, the Old Man took to going frequently to the fifth room, at the end of the landing at
the top of the stairs, where he kept his treasures.
There was a sea horse he kept on velvet in the bottom
of the box, and sea grapes, and labyrinths of coral
where flies hatched their eggs in winter. The Old
Man put bracelets of elephants' hair on his wrists.
Then, the room that was long and low and looked out
under thatch at grass, and water-meadows that were
all the time half under water, felt the rustle in the
thatch of unseen animals; and far out over the

meadows antelopes grazed, with legs as long and stiff as bulrushes. The Old Man liked this room better than any of the others in the house. Nothing had been brought into it that had died a violent death: he had made sure the skins of tigers and bears stayed on the upper floor, by the room where the statesmen gambled; and he liked to think that the yellowing sea-weed fans, chipped shells and general flotsam had somehow drifted in of their own accord. From the days when the water had been higher in the meadows, and only the tops of the downs had crested the waves, these harmless fauna of the sea had wandered into the house, to become enclosed in walls of brown water, with a roof of yellow sea thatch as covering. For the Old Man liked to think, on days indifferent to dark or light, and marked off only by the baker's van or the postman coming red or white up to the back-door, that he was just as happy to live under the sea. He was as much in water as air, and the bright buttercups just opening in the meadows scattered in shoals when the wind blew, and lay tail side up. Then, when there was no African night to come down round him, no wide sky and stars, the Old Man twisted the ring of elephants' hair on his arm and he walked on the ancient seabed. At his feet, conch shells were crumbling, and sometimes, from the roof of sodden weed, a water-snake arched, and fell.

Mr Paxton went to the fifth room, on the night his wife had shown impatience with him. Mr Paxton's feet were the first part of him visible, in the mirror. This was propped on the floor and was in a gilt frame water-logged with Victorian fruit and now encrusted with dust. He bent down, and wiped at the surface of the mirror. His black shoes came back at him, and he walked away into the centre of the room, with his feet going down in the dusty room like a man walking for the first time on the surface of the moon. He saw the Old Man – and he stopped still, facing him as he stood by the window, under the straw beard of the dilapidated roof, while the Old Man stared at him, and then turned to look out at the water-meadows, or the African plains, where dark had hidden the animals and it was hard to see as far as the river-bank.

Mr Paxton said he had come to find something for the baby.

'Something like a toy,' said Mr Paxton. He was uneasy, catering for this child whose fingers could as yet only open and close, like the most primitive forms of life. He would go soon and get himself the child he deserved and had expected, a twelve-year-old son. But for now, he held in his mind this room at the end of the landing, filled with debris from the sea. Flotsam would be recognisable to the baby, baffled as it was by the strange shapes of the new world of the earth. As the child had floated in the sea of Mrs Paxton, or bobbed in its chest on the waves as it came up the river, seeking an old king for a father, it would have known the frayed sea wool, and coral white and malignant as an inner growth. Mr Paxton bent to examine a shawl of seaweed lace, and dismissed it for not being a toy. For a certain time he even stood stupidly, with a cuttlefish in his hand. He replaced it and stood staring at his hands, which were white and bony, as if the flesh had been nibbled away.

The Old Man said there was nothing here a child could possibly want. At the same time he pointed to a basket in the corner, where he had put things he was not quite able to throw away. The Old Man indicated to Mr Paxton that he should act as proxy for the child, and put his hand in the basket. And this Mr Paxton did, drawing out a comet's tail of silk ties and a gourd and pomegranates tied up in a yellow handkerchief.

At first the Old Man, excited by the appearance of this forgotten fruit – which he had picked up, he thought, in Alexandria or in the courtyards of Granada, where the sun was red at three in the afternoon and the fruit withered instantly, shrinking, sucking itself in, and was hollow finally, with pips rattling about inside – at first, the Old Man held on to the yellow handkerchief and stood with eyes shining, back turned to the window and the watery world where he lived. He thought of the hot earth, and sun coming down through women's parasols, dotted red

and white as the insides of figs. In his dream, as he
held the pomegranate, he saw the red sun come down
on white pillars and shoot out in black columns on the
earth, as if the white temple, the crucible, had burnt
up the fire from the sun and thrown it down into black
pillars of shade. The Old Man wished he could get
away from the water-meadows, and the caterwauling
of the boys on the downs. He wished he could sit
under a pine tree, with pine needles so hot and dry
that one flash of his glass ring would set the forest
alight.

Mr Paxton had taken back the bundle of fruit and
now he was sorting which he would take, and the
Old Man opened the pomegranate for him, so those
were the seeds he sewed, in the end, into a cloth bag
on the end of a wooden spoon handle. The seeds had a
musty smell, and the Old Man sneezed as they rattled
in his palm before handing them over.

The room was dark – all this had taken place as the
last light went from the fields and the river – and it
was lower, as if it had gone down, under the weight
of thatch, into the ground. The Old Man and Mr
Paxton hurried from it. The Old Man went to the
upper landings, to see the Blue Women; and Mr
Paxton went to the kitchen, to the hiss of the kettle,
and sighs from Ella that were just out of time with it;
and Mr Paxton sewed the seeds into a little pouch, so

Alice could hear them rattle together at the lifting of a hand.

In the last days of the cold weather, when Mrs Grogan said summer was just around the corner and her daughter Ella thought immediately of the Australian winter and Bob covered in snow, the Old Man's house was scoured and cleaned. Doors opened from one side of the house to the next. Until the hot days came, scattering in the Old Man's rooms dead blossom and a film of pollen, there was a wholeness to the house which made it possible to go from one part of it to another with ease – from the rooms of the Paxtons, that were green and shining – to the newly cleaned rooms of the Old Man. The Blue Women, in the sudden respectability of the spring-cleaning, walked down from the tapestry and paid Sunday calls on the Paxtons. Their eyes were bright and indignant at Mrs Paxton's thrift. A smell of soap and water hung about them after her scrubbing. The Old Man coughed irritably when he sat with the Blue Women, and he cursed the patting and shaping that was bringing his house – long ago sprawled and dispersed into separate encampments over fields and garden, into one home. He could hardly see the necessity for it. He shuffled on the landing, ashamed when he saw his collection of famous men in corners where the cobwebs had been dusted away, or walking uncertainly in too harsh a light, curtains all removed for washing and starching, and the mystery of corridors gone at the stroke of a brush.

Mrs Paxton was happy to remove the traces of the Great Men as she made the house into a round ball, suffocating as a ball of wool. She drew thick veils of white paste over the glass, so there was no way of looking out and seeing the world. Freud's pinstripe trousers were quickly dismissed, no more than a wasp-shadow lying by the door to the third room off the landing. Picasso was more difficult, leaving as he did a mass of angles for Mrs Paxton to walk through, with Mrs Grogan trailing a mop behind her: old newspapers reared up, at the slightest gust of wind when a door was opened, and flattened themselves messily on walls, and on the sheets of the Old Man's bed were little round black curls, the curly head of a Minotaur nestling in the sheets. Mrs Paxton scrubbed on, and put down poison for rats. The Blue Women went back to the tapestry and lay still. And Molly and Pam came to visit again, reassured by the odour of cleanliness. But the Old Man hardly bothered to hear their chatter. He missed the shadowy sounds that had once been in his rooms. The Great Men, sprayed out of existence, had been his only real companions. Mrs Paxton had kneaded the house to a ball, and it was intolerable to him. Ella, as she went about the gardens still waiting for the first burst of spring, saw him sometimes at a glistening window, where it seemed the glass had come away with the dirt: he stood there exposed, raw as the new buds that were hanging from the trees.

Mrs Paxton in her usual rounds 'did' the upper landing first, and flung open the window of the eternal smoking-room. A great coughing sound went out, like pigeons from the roof at the firing of a gun. The dead lungs of the elder statesmen wheezed and clapped, and baize card tables were scoured of ash, and a thousand cigar butts, each a political deliberation of ten minutes long, were emptied in Ella's pail. Without a second's hesitation, Mrs Paxton swept red pins from the military maps on the wall. And the house closed round a world that was no longer demarcated, that lay helpless before Mrs Paxton, ruled by her sceptre of feathers, ensconced in a knitted ball. Ella raced the Hoover over ash-scattered carpet. Out by the river, where Mr Paxton stood at one stretch, in his perplexity gazing at the water, and the Old Man stood at another, the hum of the Hoover came like a swarm of bees from the highest reaches of the house.

Mr Paxton thought of fighting bees, of smoking them out of an attic where in his mind they had already stung Ella on the legs and buttocks. He went sharply to the house. Mr Paxton saw the fiery kisses on Ella's skin, and clouds of smoke in the attic. But there was no war that could be fought against Mrs Paxton's Hoover – for now he was there he knew the sound – and Mr Paxton went back to his stretch, this time taking a rod with him for the look of it. The Old

Man still stood in utter desolation, in the rushes and green swamp by the river's edge.

Mrs Paxton, now she had a child to take with her, was quick on the upper floor. She cleaned more cursorily in the abandoned rooms off the main landing, once she and Ella had gone backwards down the stairs, scrubbing and washing as they went, in a waterfall over the wood. Her hope was, now she had most of the house under her control, that she wouldn't have to go deep in the springs and mattresses of unused four-poster beds, as for some years she had found herself doing – and that, once she had banished the great artists and thinkers, and stilled the Blue Women, she would be able to return to the kitchen and feed the child. Alice was moved, along with buckets and mops, from floor to floor and from room to room. Her round eyes stared up at ceilings, which curved down to meet her gaze. Her mouth was a ring, in the great round nest of the house. And Mrs Paxton made the nest by pressing herself against walls as she scrubbed, by standing on her toes and spreading her arms as she dusted, and with her breasts pushing and battering the obdurate corners into shape.

IN ALL THIS circularity, Mr Paxton stood holding his fishing rod over the current of the river. He was aware of the house like a balloon behind him, and his rod the only straight line, a string attaching him securely to the great belly of the house. He felt he would never escape the roundness, and he even saw his child as having no other function than that of being attached to Mrs Paxton's breast. The river, swollen by spring rain, flowed at his feet over a bed of chalk, and carried along with it scribbles of black and brown fish, none of which bit at his hook. From time to time, Mr Paxton looked up river at the Old Man as if he might find a solution. The Old Man never returned his gaze. He stood staring up into the sky, at the long white clouds, and he kept his eyes averted from the swan's nest, at the possible one egg or two. He knew the long ridges of cloud in the sky would in the end curve, and that the world was a sphere, but he preferred to deceive himself, to imagine those long strands of cloud going on into infinity, parallel lines which would march him far from the maternal order, the terrible roundness of life in his ruined house.

Mrs Paxton was afraid, in those days, to let herself get out of sight of the child. She was at a loss without the eyes of Alice trained on her, like a rope of blue light anchoring her to the spot. She knew the roundness she had was precarious. So she said to Ella, when it came to a clean-out of the fifth room: 'We'd better take two buckets of water and this time we'll put the baby's basket up on a table. We don't want the underside getting wet and it would soak to the mattress.' Ella agreed, although her mind was elsewhere. She understood vaguely that if anything happened to the child, these new relations in the house would be spoiled. The newly washed curtains billowing would go flat against the windows, corners would grow dark and sharp again. She knew the fifth room, as Mrs Paxton called it, was always the worst to clean. The Old Man liked to keep his rubbish on the floor there. Once a year Mrs Paxton could get in and overcome the stale sea smell. So Ella helped Mrs Paxton prepare for the assault. There would have to be running and lunging, and the child might be at risk. They took a bucket of soapy water with them, and the baby in her basket, so that she could watch the water go down on the boards.

Far away and small, Mr Paxton saw portions of Ella and Mrs Paxton in the window as they moved into the fifth room. He saw a red bucket held aloft and felt the water run from the river under his feet and into the room, his favourite room and the Old Man's too, and cleanse with its fresh water the secrets left by the sea. It was too much for Mr Paxton. He laid down the rod on the bank, and he walked up through rushes and then over grass to the gate. Mrs Paxton turned at the sound of the gate, but he was too quick for her. In those days Mrs Paxton liked to have everyone present, and hanging from her in the house.

MR PAXTON WENT to the village on the downs. He wanted a boy, and he had decided to go and get one. Ella had heard one night in the kitchen Mr Paxton saying the garden needed a boy, and he would talk to the Old Man about it. Now he had gone to fetch a boy for the garden, to make him stand scything grass, and as the grass went down more of the boy would come into view. Mr Paxton had spoken proudly of him, long before he went to get him, and called him a lad. The boy would follow in Mr Paxton's steps.

WATER WENT DOWN on the floor, from swinging buckets. Ella and Mrs Paxton stood quite still, arms swinging, facing each other in the round face of the house like the hands of a clock. The house settled round the pendulum of their swinging arms, and from her safe perch on a table under the curved ceiling the child looked down, at the tick-tock of the minutes of water as they rose out of the bucket and spat on to the floor.

Mr Paxton, in the garden, gave orders to the boy. They stood on the grass below, on the other side of the unwashed window pane. The dust on the pane

gave a murky halo to Mr Paxton. He was pointing at
the grass – and he was also sending the boy to the
stables for wood. The boy went again and again, back
and forth from lawn to cobbles to stable. He was
carrying long spars of wood. It seemed Mr Paxton
was going to build another house, now Mrs Paxton
had made the Old Man's house uninhabitable.

A T THIS TIME every year when Mrs Paxton was at
her most triumphant, the house and the woods
and the river completely in her power, the river
turned in its course and flowed into the fifth room.
The river licked the dry sponges, and seaweed brittle
as spun sugar. There was a scraping of shells, as the
river nudged and sorted them. In the bright water,
the Old Man's pomegranates were a city of domes,
presiding over a fresco of lush meadows of sea-grass
and pebbles of stained glass. The woods, bending to
the will of Mrs Paxton on her day of triumph at the
cleaning of the fifth room, came to her tied together.
Mrs Paxton swept the floor with them, and rolled the
green turf of the downs into strips before beating. It
was the day of greatest roundness for Mrs Paxton,
and as she stood by the river in the room she sang
aloud, as if even the sky, which hung above her like a

cleaned-out ear, would come down into the room to hear her song.

In the spring of the birth of Alice, Mrs Paxton and Ella paid no attention to the hammering in the garden that was Mr Paxton and the boy. They waded in the river, with skirts tucked up, and they plunged the brooms in, so that forests of dark trees grew in the clear water. Coral made red leaves, falling to the riverbed and settling, waiting for another gale to blow them back on the trees again. As Ella and Mrs Paxton went, they took the mirror with them – the old mirror the Old Man kept always propped on the floor – for they were afraid, with so much water about, that they would walk into it and smash it to pieces.

Alice lay suspended, between the sky and the river under the table. She saw, high in the sky, caterpillars of cloud in the blue, and the Old Man reach out to them before he took the reins to stand astride the moving ridges of cloud. Ella lifted the mirror, and found a hook on the wall over the table, where it could hang safely. At first, Alice saw her father and the boy in the garden, reflected in the mirror and hammering at a platform on wooden legs. Then she saw the Old Man, dancing under the black spots of the mirror, leap from the riverbed to the long, straight flight across the sky. The swan rose, wings flapping. Ants' eggs in the nest showed white and disappeared.

The child that had been born in the mirror hung above Alice. A display of fingers escaped and fluttered in greeting. Four blue, vacant eyes wandered the room. Mrs Paxton smiled, when she looked up from her scrubbing, that she was so easily able to see her daughter reflected there, in the mirror stooping down from the wall on its string. She had no longer to go over every few minutes and peer into the sides of the basket at the child. Mrs Paxton smiled at the reflection which showed the child swathed in watery shawls, smiling back at her – or returning its own smile in the first dim blinks of consciousness of itself.

Ella and Mrs Paxton worked with greater speed after this. The river was conducted into pails, carried downstairs and emptied out black on to grass. The sea relics were restored to their spaces on the floor. And the Old Man's collection of fruit was piled on the table, where it was for an instant shown, with the view of the window behind, and the pillars and architraves of the trees and downs, as a Pompeiian painting crumbling at the sides. Then Ella propped the glass back on the floor again. With one whisking hand she took Alice in her basket and was gone. Mrs Paxton went after her, carrying the long mop with a blue handle.

As they went, Mrs Paxton looked in apprehension at the walls, and ceilings that had set stiff and square again. She stopped, after going down the long landing, down the stairs, at the door that was like a boulder to be rolled aside before escaping from the Old Man's part of the house. A tall window by the stairs showed Mr Paxton's platform, and Mrs Paxton gazed anxiously up at it. With every nail that went in to the scaffolding, she heard the grim, square ending of the house that she had tried to build.

MR PAXTON STOOD on the platform he had built, which was now in the centre of a fortress. The fortress protected the child, like a shell. From inside, the child issued orders. High up in the grey, square towers were slits; and from these the child could look out without being seen. A rain of screams came from the slits, and Mr Paxton and Ella walked about with their hands over their ears. Mrs Paxton simply shook her head. Tears flew out of her eyes at the child's commands and screams, and the tears were perfectly round, the last trace of her roundness, as they went out into the room. Mr Paxton complained that the child was crying for its white ball, lost again. He swore he would tie up the ball if it ever was found, so it could fall from the cot and bob back up at the pull of a string.

The Old Man walked about in the fortress and set up his rooms as they had been before. The rooms were cramped, dark; but the Old Man bowed to the will of the child, to the reign that was just beginning; and with good humour he sent the lad out to clear rubbish from the marshland that stretched out in all directions from the fort. He saw his own ending, and in the boy, who was called William, he saw his likely successor.

Outside, over the garden and downs where the Old Man had liked to pick out each detail of the different flowers, and the leaves on the trees that had every shape except each others' – a forest of differences with the gaps filled in by fragments of sky in a million movements and forms – there was now flat marshland, and lumps of detritus mounting in the same colour of sludge over it all. The child lay in the fortress by the mirror, and in its tyranny, its first monstrous recognition of itself, issued its commands.

As William moved about, singing the songs of the new groups that were coming out of the cities, the Old Man smiled at him. He was glad to have an amenable youth, in the grey stone fort where the rule of the first months of the child had brought vistas of nothing but spiky marshes from the narrow windows, and great piles of rubbish that accumulated again as soon as they were cleared. The Old Man told Mr

Paxton that he thought he had done very well, in finding William. He saw in his mind's eye already the wedding of Alice and William, on the scaffold Mr Paxton had ·built, and before that they could act in pageants for him, so he could watch all the ages of England roll out before his tired eyes. Mr Paxton too saw the marriage, and in order to dispose of the time that stood in the way of this, he made a coach and four from a box, and put tiny dolls inside on the way to a bridal ceremony; and he made a doll's house, where they would live later. Mrs Paxton was in charge of the dusting of the doll's house, and seeing to it that the swallows didn't come in the window and nest under the cardboard eaves. She, too, living in the stone walls of the child, looked forward to the wedding of William and Alice. Her own nest, which she had tried to stick from earth and saliva, and the glutinous tears from her eyes, had failed completely. At that time, all she wanted was to see her daughter grow up and go away. And she, too, tried to dispose of this time – by looking into the pages of magazines for brides, and trying to forget the failure of her nest, a nest of life and death, and earth, stuck together with the runny white of the sky.

As the days stretched out and the forest grew taller, the Old Man spent more time on the river bank, looking at the swan from a thin belt of trees. The marsh had grown up everywhere. Grass hardly showed under the reeds. Animals and birds hopped in twos, making the only rustle. There was no wind. He wished he could be alone, at this time of pairing. But people came to see him, in couples. Molly and Pam brought each a friend, big men in brown trousers, who stood beside him on the bank with field-glasses in their hands. Ducks and moorhens went past, beaks pointed down at reflections in the water of white-rimmed eyes and tufts of green feathers. The Old Man longed for the evenings, when he could sit under a dim light with the Blue Women and think of the time before the birth of the child. For, now the Blue Women were in the fortress, they were at last where they belonged. They belonged in the ancient walls, and were no longer imitations of a vanished age. The Old Man would stare at them for hours on end, as if they could make him forget the great split going on around him: downs that parted with new roads; tense faces looking back from mirrors at Mrs Paxton and Ella; the sharp line of the river cutting off his land from the rising hills.

'Isn't the cherry blossom nice this year?' said Molly, as the Old Man looked out in desperation at the trees serried in twos and white-ribboned. And Pam said she had hoped to play tennis, to pat a ball to a partner on the old court by the lines of trees.

'Tea for two', sang Mrs Grogan, who had come in to help with this spring party. Only the Old Man sat dejected, at the tinkle of spoons and the rhythmic rattle of pomegranate seeds, as the child waved its new toy at him.

On the occasions of the spring visits, even the company of the Blue Women failed the Old Man. In the high, stone room their faces seemed to him pinched and stubborn, and he could have thrust them from the slit windows with their long, woven hair hanging down. He put his hands over his ears, so as not to hear the banging of the spoons, or the hiss of the rattle to a new samba from Mr Paxton's radio, or the chink of dice on the floor above, as the statesmen, gambling for England and Empire, doubled the stakes and lost, and then doubled them again.

IN THE DAYS when it was still cold and grey in the Old Man's house by the downs, a postcard came for Ella from the other side of the world. But the writing was small and prickly, and made Ella cry. On the stamp a kangaroo was jumping, in front of a red sky torn at the edges with white. Over the kangaroo's stomach, where a head was looking out of the pouch, a round mark had come down; and from this the two animals bounded into the redness of the sky. Ella steamed the stamp off the postcard, and then threw it away. She ran to pick up the child, but she had been saddened by the thing, and by Mrs Grogan saying, 'Is that all?'

WHEN THE SUN came for a short time, it sealed off the Old Man's rooms from the rest of the house. They were cut off from the Old Man and there was no way of getting in. Doors opened and closed mysteriously, revealing odd shoes, and gloves piled on the floor, and sometimes a tapping leg, keeping time to a conversation. As Mrs Paxton and Ella went about the house cleaning, Alice sent screams from her open mouth in the kitchen, and the Old Man went deeper into the shawl he carried all the time now on his shoulders. He would muffle himself in it, to cut out the hail of sound from the child. He opened his hands and closed them, as if grasping at an invisible prey, at the sound itself which he wished he could crush in his fingers. The Old Man knew, however, and so did Mrs Paxton, that these screams were not yet at their height. Alice, before she fell from childhood, would be likely to give a scream so terrible there would be no mistaking it for miles around.

The child's mouth was all the time round and open. William held up to Alice the bridal box her father had made, and slid off the top, and then he took another box, a wooden one he had made himself, with a lid that raised and fell back into place, and he raised the lid and let it fall. He liked the hinges, so small he had had to fix the glue on them with a pair of eyebrow tweezers. He alternated the two boxes, so Alice's eyes rolled from side to side and up and down at the opening and shutting of the boxes.

Alice opened the box with the accidental moving and waving of her fingers, and as William stood distracted, she watched a line of sunlight come into the scrap of mirror in the lid and fall on Mrs Paxton, distant and minute by the boiling kettle. The sun moved on to the mother, a strong yellow beam that made a third leg hanging over the expanse of lengthening tiles. Then it went altogether, as the lid of the box slipped shut again and Alice's mouth still gaped open at her mother standing there: at the power of the woman with the phallus of the sun between her legs; the woman who had carried two deaths in her, her own and the child's.

The Old Man came in from the river, and said the real spring had come at last. There was some warmth in the sun. The second swan's egg was hatching, and now there would be two chicks to see. William went quickly, opening the door and running out. Ella and Mrs Paxton gasped, at spring outside the half-open door like a cloth on a line, printed with green bushes and buttercups. They put down their tea and followed the Old Man, and they all went to the river, to the swan's nest and the hatching egg.

IN THAT SPRING, the Old Man had a wary expression as he stood on the river-bank and watched Alice's lost ball, the ball of white shell break into two. He saw Love and War, and death and the resurgence of life, in the bedraggled creature from the egg, soon joined by the other on the ripple of current that went at speed past the nest. The two halves of the egg lay burnt-out on the twigs. The Old Man and Mrs Paxton and Ella stood on the bank like funerary statues set to stare out over water at sand.

M R PAXTON HEARD the tramp of Soviet troops as they went into Hungary, on his radio by the arm of the chair in the kitchen. The arm of the chair was curved and padded with a rose chintz brown from the number of times Mr Paxton had put his arm down there. Mr Paxton heard the boots all that year, marching into his radio and out again, heels and toes grinding the faces of men and flying the unwanted bomb high into the air like a football. Wherever Mr or Mrs Paxton or Ella turned, in the kitchen where the child was beginning to pull itself along the floor, and where the sun was coming in fat and round in the hot days, they heard the crashing and tramping of boots. Ella, already caught in the web of the child's own time, where each step she took was measured in a game of skips and numbers, and the Old Man was green and bearded as an old king and shut off from the Paxtons by a sheet of ice, thought herself, at the sound of the boots, in a dungeon, with warders marching her Bob off to be hung. She skulked in the kitchen and refused to go into the larder, where bowls of milk stood waiting to be skimmed, and the sun, sending in a thin white line under the door, made a Prisoners Base of the tiles. She had to grab Alice, when the child edged its way to the door of the forbidden larder, but she would go no further herself. They might fall together, under the door with the strip of light that could have been the sky there, upside down, and they would go through the floor of black stone, helter-skelter into night. Ella's movements were more confined, as the child grew. And

Mrs Paxton walked carefully. At any moment, they knew, they might find themselves flung out into the garden, on their knees by the river and arms in up to the elbow, searching for the lost ball. On the black floor of the larder a frog would hop, demanding to be carried in.

IN THOSE FIRST years of the child's life the transformations of the Old Man's house grew more acute, and his defences more desperate. The chatter of Molly and Pam was no longer enough to keep out the interference. The Old Man had his cousin to stay, a man who looked as if he had long ago died and now wandered the earth with nothing better to do than sit and chat with the still-living, in rooms where time rapped on the windows like hailstones. He talked quietly and ceaselessly into his hands, which were brown and had moles for eyes, the brown blotches of the grave. The Old Man's cousin was called George. He told the Old Man of times forgotten, and he let Ella and William sit there too so they could stare at him. He talked of people, and they came sometimes, complaining of the conditions of the journey. They were bright at first, from the challenges and traps of youth in the memories that summoned them. But they soon faded, and to the eyes of the Old Man's cousin George and the Old Man they degenerated into fragments: the angle of a cheek, or a piece of velvet in the cushion on the chair. They could not be sustained long, and the Old Man and George would go up to see the statesmen, in the windy room that filled with leaves at the ending of summer. After the past, they needed to be reminded of the actuality of things. But they found the statesmen had taken to gambling with the Blue Women, and the map on the wall was rolled tight. All night, in the winds that came with the ending of summer, they heard the ball in the roulette wheel on the floor above – and the Paxtons heard it too, in the kitchen, when Mr Paxton had switched off his radio.

IT WAS HARD to know, in those years of the growing of the Paxton's child, which came first: the scream, or the echo of the scream which swept in from the downs, or the times of the Old Man's cousin George's visits and the appearance of runnels in the water-meadows, straight chalk ditches over the fields which bisected them at equal distances. At these times, every piece of string in Mrs Paxton's kitchen went into a knot. Sometimes it seemed the child was intent on ending its own infancy, with its murderous scream; at others, that it was screaming because it wanted to stay in infancy forever and was being dragged away from it too soon. Mr Paxton looked grim, and asked Mrs Grogan for some drops for the screaming. He had no interest any longer in the marriage of Alice and William, or the tiny bridal couple with a bouquet of orange blossom he made from shreds of cigarette papers in the evening while Mrs Paxton cooked the supper. He saw his daughter as something that screamed and ejected filth into the world. For this reason, despite the deathly quiet of the Old Man's house at these times, with chairs set at right angles to tables, and even the relics of the sea in the fifth room ordered and laid out in rows, like objects in a museum, Mr Paxton welcomed George's visits and went out of his way to make him comfortable. He had a difficult task in this as Mrs Paxton disliked the visits as much as he liked them. It was simple for Mrs Paxton and Ella together, when the wild spirit of the child possessed them, to go to George's room at any time and fold back the sheet, so that his frail old legs went into an apple-pie bed. Mrs Paxton and Ella were afraid of the control that lay over everything when George came. Even the Old Man looked as if he counted each hair on his head when he combed it, before piling an equal number on each side of the parting.

George made the house a house of the dead, where people walked on narrow paths and stopped sometimes to look about them with puzzled expressions, as if they couldn't believe this is where they should be. The river outside was as flat and grey as a strip of concrete. Mrs Paxton and Ella did not want the child subjected to this, for all the screaming and cleaning up they had to put up with. In the kitchen, when the Old Man and George looked in, they made a silence, and Mr Paxton gazed at his feet in shame. For Alice, crawling in her freedom over the tiles, would leave a trail of filth after her – escaped from nappy and pants, it oozed on the rectangles of black and white, a winding river of bright shit. And Ella would say, snatching her up as George left the room with his eyes to the ceiling and the Old Man and Mr Paxton stood quite close but not looking at each other: 'Isn't it a clever little girl, then? *Who's* a clever little girl?' while Mrs Paxton pushed the mop in soapy water, and restored to perfect symmetry the black and white angles of the floor.

When there was no filth, and Ella stood crooning over the pot in her attempt to train the sphincter of the child, George stalked the house with a pleased smile on his face. He was bent on the task of complicating the Old Man's house. Frames of simple gilt round the pictures of the Old Man's brothers, and the dark painting of his dead aunts, became impossibly garlanded, with grapes and acanthus leaves shooting out of the wall behind them, as if from a hidden fountain of gold. The Old Man and Mr Paxton, when they left their different parts of the house, would find themselves converging on un-known landings, and they walked into rooms where the leaf pattern on the walls was at one moment discernible as wreaths of willow – and the next was a crazy display of white diamonds, with cracks between that showed sky of a bright green.

Mrs Paxton sighed, picking from her kitchen drawer string that had looped and knotted, and for which she had to ask Mr Paxton to pass a knife so she could cut it completely. She wanted to make a parcel, to send a sweater she had made Ella knit for her Bob, as it was winter at the other side of the world, and the threads of wool, knitted into a tender pattern, might pull him back out of the antipodes. But although the brown paper was folded smoothly, the string at the time of George's visits had always gone into a tangle. As Mrs Paxton waited for Mr Paxton to pass the knife, she would lift the ruined string to her eyes and peer at it, hoping with her eyes to travel to the inner knot. All she saw, as she stood there helpless in the kitchen with a wad of string pressed to her face was her child crouched on its round pot, a fat spider in the middle of the web.

Over the years of George's visits, the women became more strict with Alice, and waited for the house to accommodate to them in return for their obedience to it. The Old Man, horrified that this might never happen – and it showed no sign of doing so – walked in his own walls like a prisoner. In the upper rooms, Ella and Mrs Paxton no longer alluded to the sudden flights of stone steps which appeared in corners and led them down, if they were foolish enough to go, to cells without windows and a smell of dust that could be bones. They went briskly into rooms which were now inter-communicating, and had swing doors and revolving doors, and spiral staircases that led to new, higher levels where the great men lounged on beds. The more respectful the women were, the more the house became a tyrant to them. And Alice was no longer taken on the cleaning expeditions: she crawled instead in the kitchen, or, going a great distance over knobbly carpet in the Old Man's part of the house, found and spilt the inks with which George liked to draw his elegant emblems. Then, butterflies of purple and red and black rose and fluttered on the dusty floor and Mrs Paxton was called to wipe and scrub. But the stains, with their faded, accidentally symmetrical markings, were a terrible irritation to George and his precision and patterns – and when he was forced to walk over them, as he often was on his visits to the chair beside the Old Man – he ran, almost skipped – and these were the only times, in all his walking about the house, that he was ever heard to lose his measured tread.

IN THE DAYS of late summer, George had almost completely triumphed over the house and the progress of the child, and there was a sense of waiting for the scream, for some sound from her, to show she was still more than one of the automata constructed by George and now walking the passages confidently, to the terror of Ella and Mrs Paxton. When Alice went into a room, or ran out on to grass dry from the end of summer, Ella followed her to see what she would do. There might be an overturning of a table, and books and blue-and-white china plates lying on the floor. Then, Alice could read the broken china pages, the blue scrolls and leaves in utter innocence of what she had done. Or, in the grass nibbled back by the end of summer, down by the river that was low in its banks, she might scoop the mud from the side of the river and make pies, with reeds stuck in for candles and mud ready on fingers for a running dado in the house. But, whether she was in or out, she appeared hardly to know the difference. She had been taught to walk with care, and nothing broke as she went past. By the river, if Mr Paxton took her for a walk to the leaf-covered shelter where once she had fallen in her pram, she stood dazed, and came back with white socks free of mud. She played with her dolls, and put them to bed and woke them in an unending succession of days that went at the speed of the shutter on George's new black camera. Earth, water and wood were of no interest to the child. When the year began to turn, and the iron came up under the ground, that would shake the leaves from the trees and pull down the sun, Alice obeyed each law that had been set out for her. Even the leaves would fall in an ordered pattern, in a wall-paper of falling leaves, from the grey branches of the trees.

At the height of the Old Man's cousin George's powers, when each day had another hem of light snipped from it and the leaves were raked in the woods by William, and ivy and berries hung in dreadlocks on the wall by the Old Man's window, George began to take precautions to ensure that Alice would never change, would never be able to go into the next stage of life. He laid out her days in a hopscotch, with whole squares vanishing as she hopped over them, and nights coming up in a black dust on the chalk. She skipped, to the time of the shortening days. She didn't know that she might never leave George's clasp and that she would try to do so. And that was his battle, his determination to keep her forever in his rules. New wonders were invented – and she took to them with delight.

On the river, a dam was built and a pond, with a mechanical duck that bobbed its gold and green head under water, and let out a squirt of shit as it paddled to the bank. The Old Man's cousin George showed her the interior, and the workings of the compartments that operated quacking metal beak and flapping wings and paste and water solution for the shit. In the old boathouse, by the river that was now so low, he constructed an Analytic Engine, which he said could make calculations of unlimited extent. He said, 'I have converted the infinity of space, required by the conditions of the problem, into the infinity of time', and he told Ella and Alice it would answer any question they might like to ask. They could think of nothing, except to ask what they would do in the future, but George frowned at this. A few drops of rain fell, and he said it was time to go in for tea. But they saw the piece of paper which had dropped from the heavy engine in answer to their question – and it was no more than an emblem, like the complicated flourishes that were now all over the house, on pictures and on gilt mirrors on the walls. Ella took the paper, but Mrs Paxton scrumpled it up and threw it in the rubbish bin. She had no liking for George's machine, although he had visited the kitchen and promised that it would compose a sonata for her, or engage Mr Paxton in chess, and could 'simulate any process which alters the mutual relation of two or more things'. But Mrs Paxton saw already too much altered round her. She turned away from George's invitation to go to the Engine in the boathouse and listen to recorded voices, to guess which belonged to human beings and which to the computer. She was afraid her daughter's voice would get caught in there, and then the whole of the child – so that only a tape would remain, of flickering images and sound particles, in the boathouse where once there had been, harmlessly, a boat.

'I don't like it at all,' Mrs Grogan said when she came for tea and they all sat in the kitchen, with Mr Paxton expounding to William on the marvels of the new inventions. 'There's better things to do than that.'

'I'm with you there,' said Mrs Paxton, and both women saw Ella keep silent, for George the magician was able to bring her fresh pictures of the country she had left her Bob in, in a box held to the eye like a gun, and at the click of a trigger showing wide sands and mountains. Mr Paxton and William were also entranced, and spoke of the novelties they would be able to make.

'That scaffold, that we built for the village fête,' said Mr Paxton, excited over his tea, 'we can put an engine in it, and wheels, and a revolving platform.'

'And what would you need that for,' said Mrs Grogan, for she had no time for the amateur theatricals each year at the fête, the Old Man's yellow wig, and Molly and Pam singing old songs, and pots of home-made raspberry jam with paper lids blown off and wasps stuck inside. 'What do you ever need a revolving platform for,' said Mrs Grogan again.

Despite all the efforts of the women, George had made necessity of luxury, and the house was in the grip of his cunning. Even in the kitchen, where the Paxtons were usually safe from the emanations of the house – of the wandering Blue Women, in search of a renewal of martyrdom, or the statesmen who would only disturb them if they had discovered a new way

228

of settling the world, or the famous men who never addressed themselves to them – they were subjected to George's tricks and foolery. The larder, when the door leading from the kitchen was open and the yellow sun of the last of the summer was filling it, turned into a picture within a picture, a cartouche in a golden scallop. In the dimmest distance of the larder, beyond grey cherubs pouting rain on the lintel, an ark was loaded two by two, miniature animals standing on a sward of green, dancing spots of colour – the bright spots of mildew that clustered on the damp stone walls. Mrs Paxton went with irritation to close the door, but not before Alice had cried out for the picture to be allowed to stay. Mrs Paxton returned from closing the door with drips of moisture on face and hair, as if the Flood had begun with a vengeance and they would all float off together, in the house over the downs.

At those times, when nothing was natural, when everything was hybrid or strange, she and Mrs Grogan averted their eyes from Alice's new treasures, found in the garden and proudly carried in: a snail, with a silver stag protruding: exquisite, silver-antlered, securely anchored, in a tiny lump of molten silver, to the interior of the shell. Or Alice would report on the changes in the garden. But Mrs Paxton and Mrs Grogan had now taken to leaving the house by the back-door from the kitchen, so as to avoid the garden altogether and get straight on the village road.

They wanted nothing to do with the maze, which George was instructing Mr Paxton and William to build, and which was going up fast, with hedges of wrought-iron and a metal tree in the centre. Mrs Paxton and Mrs Grogan tried to stop Alice from playing there, but she always escaped them, and ran out at the sound of feet in the stone paths of the maze, and the hard rustle of skirts of beaten copper. For this cousin of the Old Man, who had gained sway over all of them and showed no signs of ever being ready to go, had peopled the maze for them as well. His puppets were tall, and gracefully clothed, and the only difference between them and real people, as far as Alice could see, was that they were attached to air and she to the ground. She ran with them in the maze, to the horror of Mrs Paxton and Mrs Grogan who had chased them out of the house on several occasions. And she refused to listen to the warnings of the women, waiting instead at night, when she was thought to be asleep, for the lights to come on in the maze, and the metal tree to shine, and the sound of iron feet in the stone paths of the maze. By this time, she was completely under the spell of the deathly cousin of the Old Man, and it would have been impossible to tear her away from him. He impelled her movements and thoughts, as if she too were a marionette and he had only, very gently and supply, to pull at the wire.

The Old Man was desolate at this new, formal arrangement of his life, and sat most of the time in his rooms at the top of the house, with a circle of books and his sea treasures around him, as if they might ward off the parterres, the gilded corridors empty and cold as Versailles, the symmetry of the mirrors, each sunburst facing each burst of the sun in identical gold spokes that never moved on the wall. The house had emptied of his companions. There was no freedom for the Blue Women in this land of measure, and they stayed quiet under the blue trees, hair in gold combs sticking up out of their heads. The statesmen had gone. The tyranny of perpetual order had banished them, as well as the forbidden future tense; and gone too were the Great Men, who could no longer stay within the confines of the games, the chequers of light and dark that came in through the windows to make an inescapable board on the floor. Molly and Pam were frightened off by the glacial air of the place. They stayed sometimes a night, sometimes not as much as that, and shrank from the marionettes, who would turn to them with such apparent appeal and feeling that it seemed George had placed a soul in the bowing shoulders, or in the jointed hand proffered in the hope of a greeting. The marionettes had too perfect a knowledge of things – and the Old Man, too, would brush past them with a shiver to go quickly to the kitchen, on the days he could no longer bear to be alone in his part of the house. He was afraid he was the last of the human phase of evolution, that the puppets were the next stage, prematurely arrived.

There would soon only be machines, and recorded, abstract intelligences. He gazed in fear at the television, which had not been long in the house, and which stood in a no-man's-land, a small room between the Paxtons' quarters and his own. Heads made of a million dots addressed him, if he happened to be passing at the hour Mrs Grogan and Ella liked to watch. He saw the dots multiply, each one grow graceful limbs and a head that danced on a wire of light straight from the all-encompassing knowledge of the Universe.

When the Old Man arrived at the kitchen, things were no better. Alice was cutting paper into strips of equal length, or handing out squares of chocolate where even the chocolate dust from the edges had been trimmed in case of inequality. Since George's coming, and the Analytic Engine in the boathouse by the river, she thought only of the property of exactly-the-same – and if Mrs Grogan, say, happened to give Alice an old scarf of hers that she could dress up in, and Ella an old blouse – she eventually threw both down in disgust, at the inability to decide which was better. At her lack of generosity and spontaneity, the Old Man showed horror. She would grow up a machine, not human at all, just as he feared. And he turned, in the shabby kitchen which looked as if no computer could ever divine where the salt was kept, or the changing position of the shoe-polish, to the comfort of Mrs Paxton as she stood chopping food at the table. Over the scores of knife marks on the rough top of the table, made by hands that slipped, that committed errors, the Old Man gazed anxiously into the face of Mrs Paxton, equally lined across the top. He wanted to see the years of mistakes, wrong turnings, moral decisions, all the afflictions and yearnings of humanity, expressed round him. In the dim, greenish room where puffs of steam came from pots on the Aga, and the flypaper had a random assortment of victims, the Old Man wanted to be told to feel at rest. Yet, as the boots thumped in Mr Paxton's radio with a terrible rhythm, the Old Man saw only a child grab at an apple, and then demand of Mrs Paxton, chopping with her knife at the table, that she create a parity. Mrs Paxton's knife went deep into the apple and a green and white froth appeared in the crack. The Old Man saw Alice's arm shoot out for the portions. But the beginning of the smile faded on his face – as he saw her counting the pips, saw her staring in fascination at the divided centre of the apple, at the pips symmetrically on each side, in the form of a five-pointed star.

WITH THE RISING wind, and leaves that blew about in the garden, and the flitting figures in the maze, patches of skirt of burnished gold and gold leaf blowing at the coming of the end of summer, Mrs Grogan decided to take matters into her own hands and end this heartless life. She would inculcate the real life. All day, with the help of William, she brushed away extravagant scenes in the house: a *trompe-l'œil* of pollarded trees, in groups of even numbers, with a central fountain; parterres; a delicately graded vista. The maze faded at the touch of her broom, but had always spun itself again by the time she turned her shoulder to look back – and in the filaments, helpless, Alice still lay. And even William, as he brushed the invisible paths of the maze, found himself drawn in pavanes and knight's moves over the grass, where the secrets of the labyrinth were revealed only at dawn and in the falling of night, in runways of glittering drops. When the leaves went flying at the prod of his broom, William saw the graceful, heartless dance of the puppets, the jerk of the wire that pulled them back to the sky.

Mrs Grogan went along the road, away from the village and the young men with padded shoulders standing on the corner outside the baker's shop. She was going to the farm. Mr and Mrs Paxton walked behind her, and Alice and William dawdling after them. A silage smell came off a wide field newly ploughed in the downs, and a field of rape made a yellow square above Mrs Grogan's head. She took them right into the farm, over concrete slabs with hay and mud stuck between. Alice jumped with William for a short time on bales of hay the rain had got at, and itchy brown grass, neither damp nor dry, walked in their socks and up their sleeves. Mrs Grogan was pulling open the door of the byre. They looked in, at the udders, the milk smell, and a xylophone of pails. Out the other end of the byre, in a pen with stout bars, stood a bull. Later, in a field a mile further down the road from the farm the bull served cows and Mrs Grogan's party stood watching. When about a dozen heifers had been covered, Mrs Paxton suggested they return to the house. After so many years in the house with the Old Man, or on the grass banks of the river outside the house, she felt out of place on this flat land belonging to a stranger. The others went gladly with her, after the sight of the heaving bull, and heifers dancing in mud that was bright and slippery as sateen.

If Mrs Grogan hoped, by telling Alice after all this of the sins she must not commit and the virtues she must cultivate, that she would somehow drag her into maturity, away from the Egyptian games that sprang up in every room, with wooden men at crossroads of wood washed blue – to suggest the sea? the sky? the rules were three millennia lost – away from the jig-saw, the marbles, the dance of hopscotch, to an understanding of responsibility, she was much mistaken. George had set traps Mrs Grogan would never be able to counter. In the maze, the marionettes parodied the earnest teachings of Mrs Grogan. In dresses and coats of iron lace, they enacted crimes and punishments. And as Alice was entranced by the absolute frivolity of their performance, Mrs Grogan's words fell on deaf ears. Mrs Grogan feared more and more that she would stay for the rest of her life in the court of the Old Man's deathly cousin George.

For all his dislike of the formal order of the house, and the artificial landscape outside, where the river had been reduced to a series of loops in the design, the Old Man began to show that he would prefer things to remain as they were rather than change. As strong as Mrs Grogan's fear of Alice's arrested development was the Old Man's not-wanting – to look out one morning and see a wilderness, with the river in spate and flowers slipping down out of control into the weed.

The Old Man went often to the fifth room off the landing, in these days. In the heavy air of the end of summer, he had to open shutters, and then windows where flies had suffocated between shutter and pane.

He looked out at the maze, the tracery of shadows of the house on the dying grass, and the downs which faced him with their round mouths, mouths as round as cannons. There was no sign of water anywhere. Behind him, in labelled rows, was his museum of the sea – starfish, the little dead houses of ammonites, sponges withered almost to nothing in the terrible dryness. The Old Man nodded in satisfaction. As Alice skipped with the new rope the Old Man's cousin George had given her, on the lawn under the fifth room, she could look up and catch him standing there, nodding over his dead and shrivelled collection from the sea.

WHEN THE WIND started to rise in the chimneys, Mrs Paxton's sister came down from the north to visit Mrs Paxton. She sat in the kitchen, and the cup-cakes Ella had made crumbled in her fingers, and gusts of wind from cracks in doors and windows pulled the crumbs along the floor. When Mr Paxton came in, there was a fantail of leaves behind him. Mrs Paxton's sister said how much more tidy the house and garden were since she last had been there.

'We have William now in the garden, of course,' said Mrs Paxton. 'And there's Ella – and Mrs Grogan likes to lend a hand in the house. But *he* likes it . . . ', and she moved her chin up to show she meant the Old Man. 'He likes it that way, now.'
'Who would ever have thought it?' Mrs Paxton's sister said.

Alice went out the back-door and over the cobbled yard to the grass. The end of the summer was there, and the shadows were black in the maze. She could see the marionettes, but they were heavy now, and knotted together on the grass. Earlier, they had danced for her: now, as Mrs Paxton and her sister sat talking of schools, of winter coats, what Alice would eat and what she wouldn't, she saw the dance coming to an end. The puppets were no longer attached, in a divine harmony, to the air and the trees and the stars that ruled their configurations. The year had gone over to the side, and the shadows were grotesque where once they had danced so elaborately. Mrs Paxton and her sister came out of the back-door, to look at the work William had put in to the garden. They crossed over to the grass and stood complaining of the lack of rain and the bad condition of the river. Mrs Paxton's sister, without knowing, stood in the maze. It was growing dark, although they had just had tea, and the shadows became even longer at her feet. Then they joined together – until they were all one, and every jerking limb or pointing shoe had sunk in altogether – in a mass grave of shadows, the night coming up in the earth from the other side of the world. Alice took her mother's hand and went indoors. On these sudden, dark evenings, with the wind moaning in the passages, she was afraid to run alone in the Old Man's part of the house. Baulked of his formal games, with the wind knocking down ivory chessmen and scattering counters from the board, George would jump out at her in the passages, head terrifyingly bandaged, and chase her until her screams brought Mr Paxton running with a broom. Perhaps the Old Man's cousin knew what he was doing when he entered into the wind and came moaning after her in the passages. Or he may have thought one game as good as another. But when he caught her, she screamed – and the Old Man put his hands to his ears at the sound of Alice's scream in the house – and Mrs Paxton said, surprised at her excitement and terror: 'Do you have to make so much noise? It's only a game of Blind Man's Buff.'

THE WIND BLEW over the downs. It scattered haystacks, and it blew away walls of pollen dust over hedgerows. In the garden, the topiary dance ended. The trees stood in a ramshackle arrangement, with limbs sticking out where leaves had been torn off. The wind brought gusts of rain. The rain sank suddenly into the grass in the night, and made a green bowl, inverted, too easy to sink in, and pulling at the legs, dragging them down into the wide, green dip. The hard floor of the maze had gone. In the place of the obscene jig of the shadows, father lying with daughter, and brother with sister, and mother with son, all the familial crimes in the whisk of the puppets' dance, there was the green of the rainy grass.

Balls of fluff – blown from trees and bushes – neither dead nor animate, wheels of white filament – flew and settled on the grass by the river. Here, it was even more dangerous to walk. The grass was treacherous, yellow under dead iris roots. The summer had ended. Mr Paxton built a bonfire of leaves. He got William to break up the rotting chair that should have been thrown out a year ago, and put it on top of the fire, with the seat, encircled with brass studs, pointing upwards to the sky.

George's visit was nearly at an end. He lingered in the Old Man's room, playing with a miniature maze only traceable with the tip of a pigeon's feather. In the fifth room off the landing, he went to inspect the collection from the sea. He waited for the sway of the starfish, the dead fish blowing up their lungs in the plentiful water from the downs. When the water came, he would have to go. George would be as useless there as an exhibit – trapped behind the waving panes of water, hair growing up in spikes, and bubbles rising at regular intervals in the sea. His mathematical precision would be of use to no one, in the sea. Only his long, white face would be left when the sea had worn him away, and weed growing off it, and barnacles, like a frame to his famous cartouches.

GEORGE WENT AT last. The scream had driven him out, the scream of the rising wind in the house and the screaming girls in the corridor, and the return of the roundness of things, and the scream from the bursting cheeks of the wind over the downs. A black car had taken him to the station. Mrs Paxton watched him say goodbye – to William and Mr Paxton, who were building a gate on their scaffold now, for a Christmas nativity play, and William and Alice crawling through it and back again for a game – and Ella and Mrs Grogan. The Old Man came out for a moment, complained of the cold and went in again. Mr Paxton came down from the scaffold, and wiped his hand on the back of his trousers before holding it out to say goodbye. 'Goodbye, Mr Paxton,' George said. The wind came between them and blew his words to the side. Mr Paxton held on to his hand and said a speech, but this too was inaudible. The wind came down on them as they stood trying to part.

Alice called out from the wooden platform where she was sitting. And everyone looked at her relieved, in the embarrassment of parting. Mr Paxton was jubilant. He had seen her point with her finger – and it was true, over the grass where the white fluff balls danced to the tune of the wind, over the cobbles zipped with moss in the cracks, rolled her ball. It had been lost so many times:
'It always returns,' Mr Paxton said.
Mrs Paxton and Ella and Mrs Grogan stood gazing

down at the ball, as if they had never seen one in their lives before.

'Of course, she's much too old for it now but it might do for a baby in the village,' said Mr Paxton when the attention had shifted to his own fierce interest in the ball. 'It just seems odd how it keeps turning up. A funny thing.'

George got into the car and drove off. He reversed on the cobbles and drove out on to the road to the village, away from the river going over its banks with the rain, and the downs and the tops of the fuzzy trees that were now perfectly round, and the house slumped as it had been when the Paxton's child had just been born. The house had been granted a respite. In this indeterminate time, when the summer had gone and the winter hadn't yet got started – when George had gone and the deadly order of the place had been blown in all directions by the wind, a short spell of childhood came back to it. George could be seen looking out of the back-window of the car as he paused at the gate for a safe entry to the road. From the oblong plaque of glass, he saw the house and the waving Paxtons standing one above the other. Alice, as if she had never grown up, was tossing her ball in the air and catching it again. And she was calling out – her mouth was round and then slack – O – a – and the vowel of cloth, in this time when everything became uncertain again, thick and indistinct, leapt above her head, to fall again, and then to rise and fall.

IN WINTER, IN the weeks of holiday that started with
the green tree and red candles, and ended in white
debauchery, the Old Man's house was stripped of
movement. The downs were stacked to a sky that let
down sheets of mist. In the house, there was a smell
of camphor balls. Mrs Paxton and Ella went about,
with the damp, cold air coming out of their mouths,
and it seemed that whatever they breathed on, fell
asleep: the Old Man dozed, in a chair set at the
window, and only woke to see trees as straight as
soldiers in the garden in front of him; Molly and Pam,
on their long winter visit, dropped off over cross-
words; and the Blue Women lay, in blue woollen
robes, in a tapestry where even the leaves had veins of
ice. The Old Man's cousin George had long gone. In
the squalls of wind that went through the woods,
under trees whipped to arches of swords, Ella played
with Alice, and William stood watching them. When
the wind dropped, and the trees stood straight again,
they all went into the kitchen, for the halves of bun
that Ella held too close to the bars of the fire. The red
leaves, still hurrying in the last breath of the falling
wind, followed them as far as the door. The red train
of leaves lay in the courtyard, waiting for the time
when the Old Man opened his door and they could
swirl in on him from the cobbles, to rise up the stairs
and fly into the tapestry. Then, the bright stain of the
leaves would bring life to the Blue Women. There
would be laughing in the house again. The hiss of the
leaves would come down to the Paxtons as the Blue
Women walked the floorboards, and they would see

the plump, white shoulders of the women in the billowing curtains by the window that would never properly shut.

Everything had changed. Mrs Paxton went to the small town and found another town had been clipped on behind it, with rows of houses and no shops. The people in the sudden new town were known as over-spill. Mrs Paxton hardly looked at them, once she had left the butcher and the chemist, and had picked up her bread. If she had to pass by the boundary of these ghostly new streets she looked away, and the children and cats that played there were no more real to her than figures in a cartoon. Mrs Paxton gazed instead at the old church on the way out of the town. The old church was on the way back to the Old Man's house, with grass that had been round it so long it climbed the walls. She knew the faces of the monsters of stone above the lintel as well as she knew anyone's; and with the new town safely behind her, she came slowly along the stretch where Alice had played when she was young – where the river almost met the road, and the trees were smocked in ivy, and Ella had said there were wolves there, from reading too many stories late at night. She saw the downs, beyond the trees, where Alice and Ella had got lost and wandered, and forgot everything except the cawing of the rooks – forgot their own names even, as they went in a circle on the desert of the downs. And she saw the wooden hut on the corner, with sugar panes and a pitch roof. Mrs Paxton's shopping bag was heavy. Mr Paxton was out with the Old Man in the car, on one of the expeditions that could end at any hour, because of the Old Man suddenly saying:

'I think it would be a good day for the sea!'

Mrs Paxton lay down by the side of the road, near the wooden hut on the corner, and fell off to sleep.

THINGS WERE CHANGING, as Mrs Paxton slept. Mrs Grogan was slapping the child, in a room with a piano no one used, near the kitchen. Alice would do nothing right, in these days. She had slipped off to the big town, with no permission to do so, and her ears wore little gold rings. They had been hiding under her hair until the time came to wash it, and now Mrs Grogan was staring at the rings as if the devil had threaded them in. The child had a red and white spotted handkerchief on her head most days too – Mrs Grogan wanted to know if she was going around as a gypsy? The Paxtons had been a long time in this part of the country, they had no need of a tramp as a daughter. So it went on. William stood grinning in the corridor, behind Mrs Grogan's back. It had been noticed that Alice gave him long glances, and also was impertinent with her father. On the scaffold, which William and Mr Paxton had built when she

245

was an infant, Alice swung daringly. She swung on the gate, and somersaulted right through – landing at William's feet if he happened to be standing there. And he often was. For all the matchmaking Mr Paxton had done in earlier years, he now looked on William with caution. It was for Mrs Paxton, this time, to persuade her husband that one day, when Alice had finished school, the two of them should get married.

Mrs Paxton slept, on a winter afternoon, in the mild air that came from the downs to the house and the river, air that hung white by the yews and holly at the side of the road. As her eyes closed, she saw holly berries and cotton-wool mist and the sun, making candles on the tree – but things were changing fast, and her vision of the old Christmas in the house as it had always been, since the Old Man's father and mother lived there and as it had been every year since she had known it with Mr Paxton, soon faded and was gone. The guitars that could be heard when the wind was in the north were plugged in now. The howl came in, hard, black blobs of sound which neither Mrs Paxton nor the Old Man could believe. Beautiful, moving pictures gave a fashion display of war, suffering and pain that Mr Paxton could summon to the table by his chair in the kitchen with a prod of his finger. Mr Paxton seldom listened to his radio now. He liked the TV pictures – but he had no wish that his daughter should dance to the new music.

In the room with the piano no one used, that was off the passage leading to the Old Man's part of the house, Ella set up her record-player. It was a red box, with a surface rough to the touch, as if the plastic box had been blistered by extreme heat. Ella and Alice danced to the music by twisting their bodies and staring at the wall ahead. When Mr Paxton came in to put a stop to it he saw them gyrating there, like the victims of a hypnotist. It was only when he wrenched the plug from the wall that they came slowly to a halt and looked about at the room, with its oblong white patch above the fireplace where a photograph of the Old Man's Aunt Maria had once hung (she in evening dress of 1913, a maple frame holding in the bustle and melon breasts: on her last visit to the house, she had removed it to her bedroom) – and the blue armchair that had gone down at the side, and the piano which no longer had anything to do with sound. They scowled, at Mr Paxton's interventions. But there was nothing he could do about the secret, alien dancing. Nor could he stop his daughter from smiling at him with red lips, lips as red as the holly berries Mrs Paxton saw as she slept, dreaming of the childhoods of winter. Mr Paxton saw a face in snow-white powder, and red, red lips. He scowled back at her, before going noisily to the kitchen and switching on the box.

In the house, at that time, there was a feeling of uncertainty. No one was sure of who they rightly were. New ideas and sciences kept the Great Men at a distance. They brooded in the upper floors of the house, where Ella and Mrs Grogan no longer went to clean, and soon it was black with dust there. The disconsolate voices of the Great Men could be heard on evenings when the river was in spate: they thought they might be properly dead now, overtaken by this new age they would never be able to understand. Mrs Grogan frowned at tales of cloned people and infants that would spring from test-tubes. Even babies would no longer be delivered in the usual way. She walked less firmly than before, for she too was unsure if the world would have a name for her, in a few years' time. And Ella was told her broken heart no longer held meaning. Ella was told, in pictures and print and diagrams and manuals that she must love constantly, and often if needs be alone – and she passed the information on to Alice on dull walks by the river, where the ground was soggy and the trees, leaden as the sky, stood like girders holding it up. Alice listened to her without surprise. Nor were they surprised when Mrs Paxton came back from her walk to the village with the look of profound uncertainty about her. For, while Mrs Paxton had been away, her appearance had changed completely. Mrs Paxton's skirt was short, right up to the knee. Her hair was short too, in layers and wisps, some of them jutting right out on to her cheeks in commas. She was more alarmed than her daughter by her different self. Alice

248

was in these skirts already, bright yellow and red, and legs like flamingoes' as she walked by the banks of the river. Mrs Paxton thought she must have been sleeping, dreaming on the way back from her walk to the shops, and some naughty boys had come along and cut off her skirts to the knee.

WINTER HUNG ON a long time to the house, where everyone slept except Alice, and when she wasn't dancing, she slept. The ground was as hard as the walls of the house, and if now and again a curtain of snowdrops came up it was soon drawn back again, into the hard privacy of the ground. The white mists that rolled in from the downs brought a bad smell with them. Mrs Grogan said it was the river that was smelling, but Mr Paxton said it was Porton Down, where they were making chemical warfare, and they would all be poisoned by the germs. He said it couldn't be the bomb, as splitting the atom was odourless. He walked in the garden, in the fog, but he couldn't even see as far as the river. Its sounds came back to him from the weir, the water crashing like an old man's snores in the white blanket that hung about the house. The fog got indoors as well, and he would bump into William standing like a ghost in the passage outside the kitchen. If William came running at Alice, flapping his arms in the thick air, she ran to the room where the Old Man sat with the Blue Women, and the fog muffled her screams.

Mr Paxton in the kitchen nodded over his tea. His eyelids were red with rubbing. If he opened his eyes he saw everything red, and when he raised his eyes to the highest window in the kitchen he saw the setting sun come through cloud, red and lopsided. He would start to complain to whoever was there about his daughter. He was certain that the power he had had over her was waning. The power had been Mrs Paxton's first, and then his, and now the girl had grabbed it for herself. Mr Paxton took his gun, and went to see if he could get a pigeon in the wood. When the mist was there the birds were invisible but they could be heard moving about clumsily in the branches. Now the sun had thinned the mist. He could see the birds, and the nests of twigs they built in the tops of the trees, and when they wheeled out into the sky, Mr Paxton fired the gun. The white mist had gone, but it would come back again. Alice and Ella ran out, to be in the thinness of the air, and the smell of smoke from Mr Paxton's gun. Those evenings, when the sun, looming over the house and the garden and the river, seemed to be about to collapse – as if it would lie like a ripped-out, bleeding organ on the grass by the river – those evenings Mrs Paxton had come to dread especially. She went about as if she were only holding herself together with great effort.

And she tried to keep Alice indoors, when the red sun first came down as far as the kitchen window. She stood looking after her anxiously when she ran across the cobbles, under creeper on the wall of the house that was as red as fire from the setting sun. She knew then, for all her gratitude that the Old Man's cousin George was no longer there, and that the days of the changing patterns of the house were over, that there was worse to come. A disaster hung in the sky before her. She saw a hole under her feet, made by the shadow of the wall in the sun, and she saw her daughter fall in, sucked to oblivion with the speed of a raft in a whirlpool. She called after her to come back, to get ready for tea. But Alice never heard her, as she ran in the wood. Sometimes she went as far as the road at the far side of the wood, where youths from the town came on motorbikes or in beaten-up sports cars. She stood on top of the wall above the road, and laughed down at them.

THE OLD MAN's Aunt Maria came to stay in this time of the year, when the sleep of the last of winter lay on the downs, and the small town had icicles hanging on the neon cinema sign, and house and river had been packed away in mist, waiting for the red sun to melt them out. Mr Paxton met her at the station. Alice watched as the car came over the cobbles and the Old Man's Aunt Maria got out. She had a fur round her neck, and at the back of the neck the vicious head of a fox, with white, pointed teeth and glass eyes. Ella told Alice she heard the fox talking to the old woman, when she went up with Mrs Paxton to take a cup of early morning tea. It had a high voice and she couldn't catch what it was saying. They planned to creep up to the room in the middle of the night, to see what really went on. They would push open Aunt Maria's door in the dark – but they were afraid to go, in case she peered out at them from under a lace cap – in case, with one bound, she was out of bed and her hairy face was looking down. It was clear, from the photograph that had been in the room with the piano, that she had been very beautiful once. Now her appearance would fill anyone with horror. Ella said she wondered why the Old Man's Aunt Maria hadn't yet allowed herself to be dead.

In that month of nothingness, of white fog that came down over downs and house, and a red sun at the end of the day, the Old Man's Aunt Maria settled herself into her favourite room. After a short time the room began to smell of her: of the powdery, old-fashioned sweets she carried in a heart-shaped tin, and the crushed velvets of her dresses, all tinged with the scent of violets dabbed on half a century ago. Her room was next to the fifth room off the landing. Alice tried to listen to her mutterings from there, standing in the Old Man's bric-à-brac of dried seaweed and shells. She could hear the snapping voice of the animal as it talked to her, and if the Old Man's Aunt Maria came out on the landing she hid behind the door, for fear of paws under the long purple dress, the wolf-shadow on the wall.

The Old Man's Aunt Maria soon fell into the habit of sleeping, and after a while she would be seen only in the candle-end of the afternoon, as she walked under the red sun by the river. Occasionally she had Molly and Pam as companions, but she disapproved of their modern ways and liked best to walk alone or with the Old Man. She told him of her mother, who had loved a great poet in 1880 and whose daughter she, Aunt Maria, might be; and her dry, old eyes lit up as she talked about passions that for long had been a pile of bones. It was the Old Man's Aunt Maria's trouble, that her own beauty had not matched her mother's, and in her jealousy of her mother she had never married. Her mother's lovers were still all she desired; and if Alice stole into her room – with William on the landing to keep guard – she stopped first at the row of silver frames, all polished by Aunt Maria at night, that held the face of the poet, or the poet standing, leaning against a plinth. She tried to love him too, to feel the dropping away of the heart that Aunt Maria must feel each time she peered at the man who could have been her father, lover, anything. But his face was too far away in time for her. The silken moustaches made her laugh. Only lines about woods or waterfalls or nymphs could be expected to come from his unfashionably small mouth. If he could have heard the music Alice played, in the room where the picture of the Old Man's Aunt Maria had once hung, he would have turned away from her in disgust.

As the house slept, and the days grew longer without anyone knowing, it seemed that a thicket grew up round the house. Thorn-bushes, red-tipped, were now suffocating the house, taking away its windows one by one. This tangle of thorns soon became impenetrable. As the house slept, Mr Paxton tried to chop down the hedge with an axe, but it came up again. Alice looked out at a red fuzz, and at night dreamed monkeys swung there, waiting to leap in. Mrs Paxton sighed, as the sun glared every evening in the kitchen window, with its rays mixed up in the fierce thorns. She blamed Aunt Maria for this bad situation. Mr Paxton said there would be scurvy if they didn't see something green soon. But when they went to the top of the house and looked out over the hedge of thorns that imprisoned them, to the downs and the meadows by the river, they could see no way of escape, and nothing green either. The fields sloped away from the house, like puddles of melted tallow. The trees were white and angular, goose feathers sticking out of the white belly of the sky. And the sky came smothering down, as they clung to the walls at the top of the house. All this until five o'clock, when the red sun made its terrifying appearance. Mrs Paxton cursed Mr Paxton and William, for not being able to chop down the hedge; and for allowing, in their ineptness, that William should be locked up in the house with them. Every day, in his captivity, he seemed to grow smaller and more insignificant.

The red sun spilt its blood, as it poked its head over the thorns and into the kitchen window. William shrank from it. Alice went often to the top of the house, to look out at the big road, just visible in the distance, where fast cars crossed the country. She was looking for a sports car, black and low with the paint bashed off the right hub. Sometimes, in the thickness of mist, she heard the roar of the car's engine, as it turned off the road and up to the house, at a speed she would never be able to refuse. She waited for it to lie suddenly at her feet, a lump of hot metal fallen out of the sky.

Down in the kitchen, where William scurried with a mop and Mr Paxton watched TV, suspicion grew over Alice's long visits to the top floor of the house. Ella was sent up occasionally, to spy. All she saw was a procession of empty rooms, with the Great Men turned to mildewed paper in this new, incalculable age, and lying about undusted on the floor or on shelves. She saw Alice standing by the window, and that was all.

Joe was the name of the man with the sports car. He was from a long way off, and he came from time to time to the small town near the house as he had a friend who did odd jobs with the forestry. Alice and Ella had seen him when they went for a walk, over the downs and on into a valley which would be planted with young firs. The car was on a steep incline of mud, with the front wheels right up in the red mud like a charger. They talked to Joe, who said he had rooms in the small town over the Axbury Arms, and they could go and see him there. He was very dark, and his nose was crooked at the tip. He smelt of haircream. Alice and Ella had been in the Axbury Arms a few times, when it was Ella's birthday and they all sat at a table on Saturday night with the band playing music for old people and Ella blushing at the shame of it. Mrs Paxton didn't like the girls to go on their own, as she had seen Italian waiters there. The lights were dim, in a decor of black imitation wood and red carpeting. Alice and Ella told Joe they would come and see him in his rooms. He said he would meet them just past the gate to the Old Man's house, on one Monday when he had been down for a visit at the weekend. They knew it couldn't be yet; the Mondays went and came as they waited; and Alice sat a long time on the upper floor, watching the swallows leave and arrive, go in and out under the roof, like needles in a frame.

IN THOSE WHITE, dead days, when the grass was still held a long way under the ground and buds on the trees were encased in iron, Alice stopped dancing altogether and slept most of the day. If she hoped to see Joe in the evening, at the coming of the red sun, she was mistaken: a line of crows might fly over the downs and she saw him for a moment in his black, battered car, going into the trees. Or she saw him on the Old Man's landing, where shadows at night made a great chariot on the wall and Joe sat inside, with his crooked nose tilted at the sky.

THE OLD MAN'S Aunt Maria had had a hut built for her by the river, when she was a child, and there was a conical roof of plaited reeds on it, and a hole in the middle, in case anyone wanted to light a fire there. The hut too was round. It was in the thickest part of the wood by the river, where the springy branches of dogwood came slapping under the eyes, and just beyond, in the white air that floated in rings, were the red spears of the thorns. The panes of the windows had been scratched out by thorns. Hearts were carved on the grey rotting wood of the door that looked every day as if it would fall off its hinges. Inside, when the door was pushed and the hinges bared to the splintering gum, there was a smell of nettles and cats' piss. Alice followed the Old Man's Aunt Maria to the hut, at times when the mist was so far down on road and meadows that it was hardly possible to leave the house at all. She pushed aside the creeper, the thicket that had grown right over the porch of the back-door and that caught Mrs Paxton's rollers as she went in and out in a fine gauze scarf. She put her hands out in front of her, in her groping way to the wood.

The poet the Old Man's Aunt Maria had loved had come to visit her mother here, when the hut had just been built. Then there had been a wrought-iron seat outside, with the back in the shape of two pigeons, iron beaks joined, in an eternal billing and cooing. The seat had gone, but the poet could be seen standing by the falling door, with his hands tucked into his pockets under a short coat. Aunt Maria had stood with a hoop, watching the poet kiss her mother and then lead her inside. Now she poked at the nettles with her stick, and stood frowning in the smelly interior of the hut. She had been too young once, and now she was too old. The Old Man's Aunt Maria fitted nowhere, and this was why she was allowed to come when there was no season to dismiss her – when Mrs Paxton cooked white food for Lent, and the red carcass of the sun hung in the mist that swirled from the river, and the snowdrops, hidden in prickles, drew sparks of blood.

The Old Man's Aunt Maria sat on the wooden bench inside the hut. Her nose jutted out almost to meet her chin. A pure beauty, which remained only in the photograph she had taken from the room with the piano no one ever used, was lacking also in the trees and river around her. The black ivy that grew everywhere was ineradicable, a black trail of corruption on naked trees and earth that would otherwise be ready for spring. The river, rising slowly after secret rains at night and edged with yellowish foam, was as dull as a cataracted eye.

When the red sun came at the end of the short day, the Old Man's Aunt Maria was lit up inside the hut, like a fetish. Alice played Grandmother's Footsteps, dodging up to the hut and back. She never saw the old woman, for she sat with her head low and her chin resting on her stick. Alice watched her float out on to the river in the hut, when the sun came down and made red, violet and orange inlets, glittering strands of light, from the mist and the thin banks of the river. The house was red. It shone red on the weightless sands, until the sand was dissolved again – by cloud, by the long arms of the downs, pulling it back into night. Then, the sequin tails of the strands faded in the river; and the Old Man's Aunt Maria, pulling the snapping head of the fox around her neck, rose and walked out of the hut. Her pointed, buttoned shoes went fussily in the ivy snares. In the last red flush of the sun, Alice ran ahead of her through the trees. Her coat was dyed red by the sun, and the prowling figure of Aunt Maria followed her to the house, her long nose and chin all one in the abrupt darkness. Aunt Maria seldom looked back, at the children's hut where her mother had consummated her love, at the red house without windows on the iridescent sands.

In these white days, which vanished into the throat of night; in these days of Mrs Paxton poaching fish in milk and taking it up to the Old Man and the Old Man's Aunt Maria, who groaned when they lifted the lid to see a white meal on a white plate, and a salad of chicory like the shavings of a young ash-plant – in these days, when the tilted sun leaked red all afternoon on Mrs Grogan's washing by the back-door, staining the bloomers red – Alice waited in the woods for the sound of the engine of Joe's car. Maybe the sound of a radio as well as the growl of the engine would come through the trees, the clumps of bamboo by the river. She heard the Beatles rasp and sigh in the tall bamboo. And she wandered in and out of the hut in the interminable waiting. Mrs Grogan was there, on the mild days when she said spring had come and she could point at the cloud overhead, thick and white as the sugar cream inside an Easter egg, lit by the yolk of the sun. She said there would be yellow flowers out any day now. And she made Alice knit, to count the minutes until darkness, on those short afternoons that were only a foreword to an endless night.

The strength of the sun grew under the clouds. Ella found frog-spawn in the river and put it in a jar. A hundred black eyes looked out from the grey membrane in the jar; but in the kitchen, where Mrs Paxton kept the jar on a high shelf, a few tadpoles wriggled free and swam slowly round, punctuating yawns and sentences. Even after dark Alice went to the hut by the river, to hear Joe's car in the rush of the weir, to hear the growl of the car in the clumps of bamboo, waiting there to pounce out. When she got back to the house, Ella's cheeks were red and she had been weeping. In all the succession of short days and long nights, her tadpole had grown into a frog and she had kept him on her pillow, dreaming of love. Now Mrs Paxton had thrown the frog out. Alice and Ella searched for it by the river in the rushes, and stuck their fingers into water-rats' round holes in the mud of the bank. The frog was nowhere to be seen. Ella shone a torch on the river and wept again, at her own distorted face looking back at her, in a tangle of last year's weed.

JOE'S CAR CAME, after a hand of white years had been played out. It came in the days of spring when the mist had gone and the sun was yellow, but the grass by the river was still swollen with rain. Joe took Alice and Ella to the rooms over the Axbury Arms which he had kept a long time, waiting. He took Alice into the furthest of the three rooms and he said Ella could make herself a cup of tea in the kitchen. Out of the window in the kitchen Ella could see the church Mrs Paxton walked by on her shopping trips to the small town. She could see the High Street, and the newsagent's that stuck out on the corner, so that a lorry had finally crashed into it one night and they had built it up just the same. At the far end of the High Street was the beginning of the new town: with the new black tarmac on the road it looked as if it was the only place to have had the rain.

AS ELLA WATCHED the streets where the rain had been, and Alice and Joe were shut away from her by two walls of peeling paint, Mrs Paxton watched the hole where rain had collected outside the back-door of the kitchen: the shovelful of black water that lay between the cobbles and the door, in the crevice Mr Paxton would never get round to mending. In the triangular expanse of water, she saw Alice fall into the arms of a stranger with black hair. She turned to Mrs Grogan, who had come out to string up some washing after the rain, and she said: 'You know, I can't help wondering where the girls are today!'

Mrs Grogan pegged the Old Man's shirts with their ludicrously long tails on to the line. She was used to this kind of thing from Mrs Paxton in these days, and if she knew where they were she wouldn't say so. Mrs Grogan seemed quite unaware of the chasm of black water just under her feet, as she leaned forward to peg the shirts. She knew Mrs Paxton was staring into the depths at the triangle of water like a witch's hat and Alice caught in it, whirling on the rim. A wind got up and a line of shoulders shrugged at Mrs Paxton. Then the shirts filled out altogether, and beat the women in at the back-door. Mrs Paxton muttered in irritation, at her vision gone. But what she had seen was enough for her: in the reflected glow of the red sun in the puddle, in the ripples that pulsed in the water at the first touch of the wind, Mrs Paxton saw the lights of evil and decline. She turned to Mrs Grogan again and said, 'We better leave the socks for later then.' And she closed the door. She turned back from the black night lit with neon, the glittering street where Alice wandered, lost, in the red sun on the black water in the hole.

ALICE AND JOE came out of the room and called Ella and they went downstairs to the dark red inside of the hotel. Drinks were set down, with cherries and orange in them. Alice said she would like to go to that part of the young wood where she first had seen Joe. He said the trees were tall now, after the years of growing. He said they were much taller than she was and very dark, because they were conifers, and she might think she was surrounded by a whole army of aunts.

'I'll get away from them,' Alice said, laughing. And they went to the car, which was still the same car, but more crumpled and with paint off everywhere. They drove out of the small town, past the Old Man's house, and on to the road over the downs, to the valley that belonged to the forestry.

In the rain that had ended the white fog of winter and rinsed the red sun from the sky, the Old Man and Mrs Paxton went about the house, talking about spring-cleaning. Mrs Paxton's face was grim and lined. She had heard the roar of Joe's car outside the gates at night, and she had dreamed of leopards. She told Mrs Grogan and Ella they would have to help with the clean-up. They all took bright plastic buckets, to the top part of the house, where spiders had caught the works of the Great Men in their gigantic webs, and to the room where the Blue Women sat, looking out in disdain at Joe's car lurking under the bushes by the gate; and to Aunt Maria's room, where Aunt Maria sipped tea by the silver-framed picture of herself as a young girl. Mrs Grogan and Ella went into rooms only visited at this time of the year. They beat untrodden carpets, whisked dusters at portraits so seldom seen they had lost their gender altogether, and could have been lord or lady under the bouncing wigs. Mrs Grogan and Ella looked into the fifth room off the landing, and decided to ignore it until summer came. For the rain had washed into the room, and the Old Man's sea collection had filled out once more. The Old Man put a small glass panel in the door, so he could show guests his marine room in the middle of the house.

As Molly and Pam stood with their eyes to the aperture, and flying horses went past, and sea anemones waved in the room of clear water, Mrs Grogan and Ella thrust mops into buckets and went at walls and landing. Mrs Paxton crossed their line of vision from time to time, as she climbed up and down from the top floor, with remnants of the Great Men in her hands. She never smiled, in those days. She thought of the early years of the child, and the care in carrying the crib to all the rooms as she cleaned them. Now, she threw the books of the Great Men into the rubbish pile by the back-door. In the damp, the books had sprouted green bindings. Her daughter had learned nothing from the Great Men. In her bitterness, Mrs Paxton lit a fire of the pile, and the smell of the smouldering books rose in the house, and went out as far as the road.

MRS PAXTON MUST have known what would happen on the day her daughter fell for the last time and disappeared from her sight altogether. She begged a lift from Mr Paxton, although her cleaning routine had only just begun, and she directed him urgently to take the road over the downs, and to turn into the valley where the Forestry had planted firs. Mr Paxton drove at an unusual speed – and the Old Man and Molly and Pam looked out in surprise from the window of the Old Man's room.

Mrs Paxton arrived at a clearing in the new forest where Ella was standing with a group of foresters. She was gasping for breath, as she had told Mr Paxton to draw up at the side of the narrow road and she had run the rest of the way along the track. The soles of her feet were red with pine needles. Mr Paxton came up too, swinging his car keys. He was not so appalled yet, though he looked round with certainty – the certainty of seeing no one he wanted, in the desolate clearing. As they both rotated, they saw the piles of fresh red earth, the yellow bulldozer above the crater it had made – for a woodman's house was to be built in the clearing and in this hole the foundations would go.

Mrs Paxton went to the side of the hole, and looked down. She saw a river of red earth leading from the pit, and she saw a lake, which had been formed by the rain pouring down before the men could start work. She knew Alice could not possibly be there. But even when she had asked Ella, and Ella had admitted that Alice had gone to London with a man called Joe in a black car, Mrs Paxton still looked down into the mouth of red earth. After a while she straightened up, and she and Mr Paxton went back to the car on the road. They said they would drive Ella to the Old Man's house.

In the next days, Ella helped Mrs Paxton prepare herself for her journey to London, where she would search for Alice until she found her. William carried the buckets up and down the house, and Mrs Grogan cursed as she did her perfunctory cleaning. William's face was long and white. No one went to the Old Man's part of the house, for fear of his cold-heartedness at the snatching of the Paxtons' daughter. He had to come to the kitchen to find bread, or an egg to boil in a kettle himself, as he had at the time of the child's birth. At night, as the preparations for the departure went on, the Paxtons heard the Old Man's long, muffled conversations overhead with Molly and Pam. The ice he had scratched from the tray with his nails crashed in their glasses, and the spring rain came down on his porch by the back-door in icy stones.

Mrs Paxton was gone a long time from the Old Man's house, looking in London for her daughter.

The Old Man was beginning to fail. Even with the coming of spring he no longer got up – and Ella had to take him trays of food, with primroses squashed in an eggcup for decoration. The primroses, which had come up everywhere since Alice disappeared, made an unhealthy glow under his chin. And Mr Paxton had to read aloud to him in the evenings, instead of watching TV or watching Mrs Paxton put on the supper. With Mrs Grogan cooking, meals became eccentric and far between; and in the winter when Mr Paxton was told by the radio that there were only three days to the week and power cuts made days shorter and nights longer, he said he was driving to London himself, to bring his wife back. He set off, with the Old Man too weak even to get to the window and re-call him.

It was Ella who found Alice, and by mistake, as she had been sent to London to go to the sales for Mrs Grogan. It was in Soho that she saw her, walking down the street in a flowered skirt, with Joe, a shoulder bag swinging between them. She went with them to the hotel where they lived, over a fish bar. The room was small, and looked out the back on rubbish in black bags almost as high as the building. Ella told Alice her mother was in the city, going from job to job as a nurse for other people's children, searching the streets for Alice at night. Alice cried, but she said she wouldn't go home. She said she belonged to this place, where it was as bright as day all night, and the days were all grey, with grey houses, and grey, mottled sausages hanging in shops, and dusty, grey trees in Soho Square. The season of high summer, just falling on the neon beds of Soho, couldn't pull her back to the Old Man's house. The season that clawed back its possessions, reclaiming its legacy of flowers and grass after a bare winter, couldn't spring her from the magnetic circle of Soho.

Ella went with Alice from the dark door of their room down the stairs and out past the stench of fish to a place where they could eat cakes and drink tea. Alice said everything had happened to her that was written in the book of the underworld; and now she knew that world and she could live in it, and she leaned back on the banquette like a queen of the shades. Joe was a pimp. First, Alice had modelled and her face had been in the magazines bought by Molly and Pam, but her own mother wouldn't have recognised her. She had fallen ill and she had gone out on the streets. And all this Alice said as the red lights of the strip shows blazed like a field of poppies behind her, and the first cottonseed of summer, blown in from the country perhaps, landed on the table by the door of the café and made an old woman sneeze. She took Ella back to the dim hotel – Joe had gone out by then to see to the rest of his business – and they went into Room 5, to the grease of the bedspread and Joe's Italian shoes sticking out from under the bed like a murderer. Ella told her of the room of the sea in the Old Man's house, a fifth room different from this, and Alice laughed in disdain at the memory of the shells. But Ella told her too that the room was filling with water again, and the Old Man was dying, and Alice put her head in her hands.

'I can't leave here, Joe would kill me,' she said. And, 'But I like it here. Can't you see it's where I belong?'

Ella left her, for she had to get home to her mother that night. She would tell Mrs Paxton nothing, and if mother and daughter came slap up against each other in the street, that would be a different thing.

It was Mr Paxton in the end who took his daughter back. On his first trip to London, the trip to carry off his wife from the child she looked after, Mr Paxton came to a halt at a red light in Piccadilly. He looked round him, at the hoardings which might have been in a foreign language, and the people giving up their life at the foot of the statue of Eros, and the ill-placed god of love flying in the grey air. Then he saw his daughter, on heels as thin as a spider's legs and with a gold anklet that made every eye look down, cross the street at the lights. A dark man walked just ahead of her, and then disappeared into the crowds.

Mr Paxton leaned his head for a moment on the steering wheel, for he was a nervous man. He closed his eyes, and in the blackness he saw the river as it had been on the night Alice was born, the black river that had brought the casket up to him and had then gone away into sea. The man who had come to claim his daughter was somewhere in the crowd around him. Mr Paxton remembered his face, as he had seen it on the night Mrs Paxton lay groaning in bed. He looked up. The cars blared horns behind him, at the changing lights.

Mr Paxton with his left hand opened the passenger door of the car. He didn't know why he did, nor why Alice walked over to him in the bellow of noise from the cars, and fell into the seat at his side. She looked tired, and he said nothing. Now there was only the mother to bring back in, and the drive away from the red lights in a sky that was perpetually light.

THE OLD MAN died at midsummer. After Alice's wedding, Alice and William would help with the conversion of the house into a hotel. Mr and Mrs Paxton would run the hotel, which was owned by the Old Man's cousin, who lived overseas, and Ella and Mrs Grogan and William and Alice were the rest of the staff. Already, the Blue Women had been sent to a sale in the county town. Molly and Pam were no longer welcome, with their suggestions for decor, and Mrs Paxton, who wanted it all as plain as possible, made it clear she would take no orders from them. In the Old Man's Aunt Maria's room there was a new paper of grey and white Regency stripe and the old photographs had gone – but Alice and Ella, as they shifted her dusty furniture for William to take out and throw on the pile, would sometimes see Aunt Maria running round behind the stripes. Her nose was as pointed as ever, and her chin played chords on the bars that imprisoned her. But Alice said nothing about seeing all this, and nor did Ella. Alice's wedding dress was in preparation downstairs. She and William would live in the room near the kitchen, where there had been a piano no one ever used. Now, a coat of shiny paint covered the walls, and the oblong patch that had been under the photograph of the Old Man's Aunt Maria as a young belle was gone for good.

The fifth room off the landing had been painted blue by Mr Paxton, in memory of the sea it once had housed. Ella had taken to painting and she added a mural, like the mural in the bar of the Axbury Arms, of goldfish chasing each other's tails and a whale spouting. Mrs Paxton said it would be one of the dearer rooms, as it had a good view of the downs. She offered it to William and Alice for their wedding night, before they went off on honeymoon.

After the wedding, at that time of late summer when the ground throws up weed and stale grass and bindweed as quickly as possible before tucking in for winter, Alice and William posed for photographs outside the church. They were up to their waists in nettles and hay. Mr Paxton threw a small packet of confetti, which vanished immediately in the greenery, and they walked on, to the back-door of the new hotel. The scaffold Mr Paxton had built when Alice was a child was still in the cobbled courtyard, and the couple stood up on it for more wedding photographs. The photographer tried to make Alice smile a little more, with her eyes which were sad and dull. But she only frowned at him, as if his reflection of her on the day of her marriage was an unimportant one.

The sun came out as the last pictures were being taken. Alice's white dress shone, and a pool of shadow lay under her feet, at the base of the scaffold. In the black shadow, which began to dance as the sun was snatched by clouds and then freed again, came the marionettes of childhood. They danced Alice's future, over cobbles always wet from rain in that bad summer. Mrs Paxton clapped her hands and called for a wedding group with all of them, and Mr Paxton and Mrs Grogan and Ella climbed on the platform, and Mrs Paxton last of all. As she laughed and blinked at her daughter in the flashes from the bulb, the sun went in and a cloud came over from the downs. So Mrs Paxton never saw the dance of the shadows under the wedding scaffold. The days that Mrs Paxton would lose her daughter, the months of white days frayed at both ends by the night – the white days that turned to red when Alice would be sucked to the streets again, neon red days in the last rays of the sun on the wet cobbles – all these Mrs Paxton failed to see as she stood and posed, in an old hat of Molly and Pam's she had found in a cupboard. With the sun gone, she and Mr Paxton and Mrs Grogan and Ella stepped down and began talking of icing, and marzipan, and tea.

Alice was the last to go, as William had bounded down, relieved to have the whole thing over. She stood on a while longer, holding her hands demurely on the skirt of her white wedding dress . . . and yet, it seemed suddenly as she turned and went towards the steps, that she swayed and was about to fall. Mrs Grogan, who was handing strong tea, shot a mid-wife's look at her on the scaffold and she said the weather was close, it was a close day for getting married in. And so they continued as before. The wedding party wandered on the grass by the river and looked at the weed, sickening with foam, that lay by the banks. They went back to the kitchen, and Mr Paxton let Ella put a record on her record-player so they all could dance. Mrs Paxton sat smiling, as if she hardly could believe her happiness.

ALICE WENT UP to the fifth room to change from her wedding dress, and Ella went with her. It was nearly dark outside, and in the half-light it seemed the room was under water once more – that water was pouring in, through the open windows, from the green reservoir of the downs. The sky was clear, though, and there were a few stars. Alice looked up, and so did Ella, as if they might see her own spangled figure hanging there, as if the only way of escape was on that trapeze of beaded light. But there was nothing there, in the space between the stars.

Ella and Alice stood by the window, until the moon unpicked the wedding dress and the stars went behind clouds. They stood in blackness, in the world of their own making: water flowed round them, in the room round in blackness. Ella's face hung above Alice, as round and foolish as the moon.

In the window, Alice's life played, in the stabbing colours of blind sight. She saw summers in the Old Man's house, and William and her mother, and clumps of forget-me-not in the long rushes by the river, in the blue flashes of comets' tails dancing into her eyes. White summer grass ribboned the black sky. And she saw the winter months, ruby streets where she would be drawn to live at the time the ground by the river was as hard and grey as stone. And she turned to Ella. There was nothing to say. Ella pulled at hooks and eyes with cake-y fingers. They both knew, with the ending of summer, that Alice would soon be gone. At the sequin-fall of the wedding dress she would step out of the ring and go. Then, Mrs Paxton and William must set out to search the forest for her – and Alice would never be there, in the artificial clearing, in the red hole in the earth her mother had first looked down so anxiously, for signs of her fall.